The Encounter

<I don't know what's happening to me, Rachel.>

"What do you mean, Tobias?"

<Rachel . . . I don't even remember what I looked like. . . >

"Tobias, someday the Andalites will return. If they don't . . . When they do come back, I know they'll have some way to return you to your own body."

<I wish I was sure,> I said.

"I am sure," she said. . . But I could see the tears that were threatening to well up in her eyes as she lied.

Like I said, hawks don't miss much. . .

Even the book morphs!
Flip the pages
and check it out!

Look for other ANIMORPHS titles
by K.A. Applegate:

ANIMORPHS

The Encounter

K.A. Applegate

Hippo

Scholastic Children's Books,
Commonwealth House, 1 – 19 New Oxford Street, London WC1A 1NU, UK
a division of Scholastic Ltd
London ~ New York ~ Toronto ~ Sydney ~ Auckland

First published in the USA by Scholastic Inc., 1996
First published in the UK by Scholastic Ltd, 1997

ISBN 0 590 19354 6

Printed by Cox & Wyman Ltd, Reading, Berks.

10 9 8 7 6 5 4 3 2 1

For Michael

The author wishes to thank the Raptor Center at the University of Minnesota. Anyone interested in learning more about the Raptor Center and birds of prey in general can contact the Raptor Center web site: www.raptor.cvm.umn.edu

Chapter 1

My name is Tobias. A freak of nature. One of a kind.

I won't tell you my last name. I *can't* tell you my last name. Or the name of the city where I live.

I want to tell you everything, but I can't give any clues to my true identity. Or the identity of the others. Everything I will tell you is true. I know it's going to seem unbelievable, but believe it anyway.

I am Tobias. I'm a normal kid, I guess. Or used to be. I used to do OK in school. Not great, but not bad either. Just OK.

I guess I was a dweeb, kind of. Big, but not big enough to keep from getting picked on. I had blond hair, kind of wild because I could never get it to look right. My eyes were... what colour were my eyes? It's only been a few weeks, and already I'm forgetting things about being human.

I guess it doesn't matter, anyway. My eyes now are gold and brown. I have eyes that look fierce and angry all the time. I'm not always fierce or angry, but I look that way.

One afternoon, I was riding the thermals, the upswelling hot air. I rode them way up into the sky. The bottoms of low clouds, laden heavy with moisture, scudded just a few metres above me.

I looked down and focused my laserlike eyes. My fierce eyes. I could still read — I hadn't forgotten how to do that. I could see the big red-and-white sign that said: DEALIN' DAN HAWKE'S USED CARS.

I pressed my wings back, closer to my body, and began to fall.

Down, down, down! Faster. Faster!

I fell through the warm, early evening air like a rock. Like an artillery shell falling towards its target.

All was silent except for the sound of the air rushing over the tops of my wings. The ground came up at me. It came up like it was trying to hit me.

I saw the cage. It was no more than one metre on each side. In the cage was a hawk. A red-tail.

Like me.

The large man was close by. I recognized him because I had seen him on his TV commercials. He was Dealin' Dan Hawke. He owned the car dealership.

He was the one holding the hawk prisoner.

She was a mascot. On the commercials he called her Price-Cut Polly. It made me sick. It made me furious.

I saw the camera. There were three guys standing around. They would be shooting a live commercial soon. I didn't care.

Dealin' Dan went to the hawk's cage to feed her. It was locked with a bike-style combination lock. Four numbers. I could see them as he turned the combination. 8-1-2-5.

I was two hundred metres up, plummeting to earth at a hundred kilometres an hour. But I could see the numbers as he turned them. And the human part of me, Tobias, could remember.

He opened the cage and tossed in some food. Then he closed it again and spun the lock.

Brilliant lights came on. He was starting the commercial. It would be live on TV all over the area.

What I was planning was insane. That's what Marco would have said. It was one of his favourite words. Insane.

I didn't care.

3

A hawk was in a tiny cage, being used as a prop for some car dealer. That wasn't going to go on. Not if I could help it.

"Tseeeeeeeer!" I screamed.

Seven metres from the ground, I opened my wings. The strain was terrible. I absorbed most of the momentum and used the rest for speed. I shot across the parked cars to the cage.

I landed on the bars and grabbed on with my talons.

I used the hook of my deadly sharp beak to click the first number into place.

"Hey! What the — " someone yelled.

The bright TV light focused right on me.

"Well, ladies and gentlemen in TV-land," Dealin' Dan yapped in surprise, "I guess we have a bird trying to break into our Price-Cut Polly's cage. Boys, you better shoo him away."

Yeah, right. Shoo me, I thought.

I clicked the second number. There were people coming for me. I saw a mechanic swinging a long steel wrench. But I wasn't going to leave without freeing this bird.

Hawks do not belong in cages. Hawks belong in the sky.

But they were all around me.

"Get him, Earl! Hit the thing!"

"Look out for that beak of his!"

"Maybe he's got rabies!"

4

WHAM!

The mechanic swung the wrench! It barely missed my head. I was dead if I didn't get some help. Fast.

<Rachel?> I cried silently with my mind. <Rachel? *Now* would be a good time!>

<Sorry! I missed the first bus. I just got here!> Her voice in my head. We call it thought-speak. It's something we can do when we morph.

I breathed a sigh of relief. Help was on the way.

"HhhuuuurrHHHHEEEEEAAAAH!"

"What in the world was — " the mechanic cried.

I knew what it was. It was Rachel. Pretty, blonde Rachel. Although right at the moment she wasn't pretty — impressive, but not pretty.

BOOM! Cr-u-u-u-nch!

"Oh. My. Lord," Dealin' Dan gasped. "Forget the bird! There's an elephant stomping over the convertibles!"

I would have smiled. If I'd had a mouth.

I finished turning the lock. I yanked open the cage door.

The hawk was wary. She was a true hawk, with only a hawk's mind and instincts to guide her. But she did know an open path to the sky when she saw one.

5

Out she came, in a rush of grey and brown and white feathers. She didn't know that I had freed her. That kind of concept was beyond her thinking. And she felt no gratitude.

But she flapped her wings and rose into the air.

Free.

And right then I had the strangest feeling. Like I should go with her. Like I should be with her.

<Can we get out of here now?> Rachel asked.

She was bellowing loudly, tossing her big trunk around and stomping various cars. Having a very good time, by elephant standards. But it was time for us to leave. For Rachel to resume her human form.

I looked up again. I saw the sunlight shine through the hawk's red tail. She flew towards the setting sun.

Chapter 2

<I hear sirens,> I said urgently.

<I hear them, too,> Rachel snapped. <I have ears the size of quilts. You think I can't *hear* them? I'm morphing as fast as I can.>

<I just hope it's *real* cops. Not Controllers.>

We had reached a patch of woods behind Dealin' Dan's car dealership. It was really just a few scruffy trees between the car place and a convenience store.

I watched from a low tree branch as Rachel morphed back to human again. If you've never seen someone morph, you have no idea just how incredibly weird it is.

When she began, she was a full-grown African elephant. Three metres tall. Almost twice that

7

from head to tail. She weighed at least three thousand kilogrammes. I say "at least" because we've never exactly tried to stick her on scales.

She had two curved tusks, each about as long as a child. And a trunk that dragged the ground when she walked and could pick up a big slashing, yelling, dangerously angry Hork-Bajir warrior and throw him seven metres.

I'd seen her do it.

<Tobias, you could at least have waited till he was done broadcasting that commercial. Thousands of people saw that on TV! Thousands!>

<Most people will figure it was some kind of a stunt or a trick,> I said.

<Most people, maybe. But not Controllers. Any Controllers who happened to be watching will guess right away that we were not just animals.>

Controllers. There's a word you need to know. A Controller is anyone with a Yeerk in his head. Yeerks are alien parasites. They are evil little slugs who live in the bodies of other species and enslave them. All the Hork-Bajir are Controllers. So are the Taxxons.

So are more and more humans. Human-Controllers.

As I watched, Rachel began to shrink. The ropy tail was sucked up like a piece of spaghetti. Her trunk grew smaller.

8

Blonde hair began to sprout from her massive grey forehead. Her eyes wandered across her face towards the middle. The vast leathery ears became pink and small and perfectly formed.

<The others are going to yell us out big time, aren't they?> I said.

<Oh, yes. I think we can count on that.>

<It was my idea. I'll take the blame.>

<Oh, shut up, Tobias. Stop being all noble. Besides, it was amazing fun stomping those cars!>

She was small enough now that she could stand on her hind legs. As she did, her front legs grew smooth and human. Her back legs lost their clunkiness and became her own long, coltish legs.

Her morphing clothes, a skintight black leotard, emerged.

The tusks *shlooped* back into her mouth and divided into sparkling teeth. She was a very pretty girl, beautiful even, except that she still had a metre-long grey nose.

At last the trunk seemed to roll up and became a regular nose.

She was a girl again. Barefoot, because no one had figured out how to morph shoes. Her mouth was back to normal. She spoke in her normal voice, no longer in my head. Thought-speech is only for morphs.

"Ok, I'm back. Let's go!"

The siren sounds were coming ever closer. <Head for the convenience store. I'll go up and look around.>

"I hope they have some flip-flops for sale in there," Rachel grumbled. "This shoe situation is a pain."

The elephant was gone. The girl had emerged.

See? I told you it would be hard to believe.

It began at a deserted construction site, when we found the crashed spaceship of an Andalite prince. He was the last surviving Andalite in our solar system. He and his fellow Andalites had fought a great battle to drive away the Yeerk mother ship.

They fought and lost.

And now the Yeerks are among us. And they are now trying to enslave the human race.

Before he died at the hands of the Yeerk leader, a terrible creature called Visser Three, the Andalite gave us a great gift — and a great curse.

The gift was the power to morph. To absorb the DNA of any living animal and to become that animal. Never before had anyone but the Andalites themselves been given the power to morph.

It meant a life of secrets. Of terrible danger.

The Yeerks think we are actually a small band

of escaped Andalites. They know that morphs had attacked their Yeerk pool. They know that morphs had even infiltrated the home of one of their most important Controllers — Chapman.

But they don't know that we are just five normal human kids who'd been walking home from the shopping mall one night.

Visser Three wants us caught or dead. Visser Three usually gets what he wants.

But I was glad to fight the Yeerks. Maybe I just had less to lose than the others. Or maybe something about the lonely, defeated, yet courageous Andalite prince touched me so deeply that I could never regret fighting to settle the score.

But there has been a price to pay. You see, there is a limit on the power to morph. You must never remain in a morph for more than two hours. If you do, you are trapped.

Forever.

And that is the curse of the Andalite's gift.

That is why, when Rachel finally returned to her human body, I didn't.

It would take Rachel a while to get home on the bus. I travelled a little faster. So I had time to waste.

The sun was setting, and in my mind I could still picture the freed hawk heading into the sun.

I hoped she had found a nice patch of forest to spend the night. That's what a red-tail likes: a

11

nice tree branch with a clear view of a meadow full of little mice and rats and shrews and voles as they scurry below. That's how we . . . they . . . hunt.

I headed towards the tall buildings of downtown. I caught a beautiful thermal that billowed up the face of some skyscrapers. A thermal is like a big bubble of warm air. It rises beneath your wings and makes it effortless to just go soaring up and up.

I caught the thermal and went shooting up the side of the skyscraper like I was riding in a power lift.

A lot of the offices were empty, since it was Saturday. But around the sixtieth floor I saw an old man looking out the window. Maybe he was some big, important businessman, I don't know.

But when he saw me he smiled. He watched me soar up and away. And I knew he was jealous.

I was a kilometre up when I finally turned away from the sun and headed towards Rachel's house.

The sun was going down. The moon just peeked over the rim of the world.

Then, I felt . . . I don't know how to describe it. It was in the air above me. Huge. Vast! Bigger than any jet.

I looked up. But there was nothing there.

And yet, I felt it in my heart. I knew it was up

there. Coming towards me, but maybe about two kilometres higher than me.

I focused all the power of my hawk's eyes on the sky.

A ripple!

That's what it was. A ripple. Like the ripple you make throwing a stone into a calm pond. The faint twilight stars flickered as it passed by. The sun's light bent. And for just a split second I was sure I could see . . . something.

But no. No. It was gone.

If it had ever really been there.

I tried to follow the hole in the sky, but it was moving too fast. I tried to see which way it was going. And where it had come from. It seemed to be moving away from the mountains and picking up speed.

But I lost it over the suburbs as it accelerated away.

I flew on to Rachel's house. I watched as she got off the bus far below me. The others, Jake, Marco, and Cassie, were all up in her room, waiting for us. I was not surprised.

<Hey, Rachel,> I said, floating above her.

She could only wave up at me. You can "hear" thought-speak when you're human, but you can't make thought-speech.

<I predict Marco's first words will be "Are you insane?"> I told Rachel.

13

She gave me a little wink.

Rachel went in through the front door. I flew in an open window. There we were, all together, the five of us: the Animorphs.

The other three of us must have seen the commercial and were not at all happy.

Marco started the conversation.

"Are you INSANE?!!" he said.

Chapter 3

Marco yelled for a while. Jake made us promise never to do something that stupid again. And Cassie, being Cassie, got everyone to make up and be friends again.

"We aren't supposed to be rescuing animals," Marco said. "We're *supposed* to be rescuing the entire human race from being enslaved by the Yeerks."

<I thought you didn't want to save the world, Marco,> I pointed out.

He scowled at me. But there's no point in scowling at me. With my face I can out-scowl anyone.

"You're right," Marco said. "But since all of you guys think you have to save the world, and

15

since you're all my friends, more or less, I just figure someone has to keep you from being *total* idiots."

Marco is the most reluctant of the Animorphs. Although actually he's the one who came up with the word "Animorph." And he's been in with us from the start. Marco just thinks we should look out for ourselves and our own families.

Marco and I will probably never be very close. He's a typical smart-aleck kind of guy. Always confident. Always has some funny or sarcastic thing to say. He's short, or at least he's not very tall. I guess girls think he's cute because he has this long brown hair and dark eyes.

Jake grinned at Marco. "So you're the one who has to rescue all of us from being idiots?"

"Boy, if Marco's the sensible one, we're all in serious trouble," Rachel said.

Everyone laughed.

Jake gave Marco an affectionate punch in the shoulder. "Just the same, it's nice of you to want to save us all. It's almost *sweet*."

Marco made a face and grabbed one of Rachel's pillows to throw at Jake.

Marco and Jake are absolute opposites, although they've been buds forever. Jake is big. Not football-player big, but solid. Jake is one of those people who are natural leaders. If you were ever trapped in a burning building, you would turn to Jake and ask, "What do we do?" And he would have an answer, too.

You can tell he and Rachel are cousins. They're both kind of determined people.

"I have to get going," Cassie said. "I have horses to feed and birdcages to clean."

"Don't say the word 'cage' around Tobias," Marco said. "He'll do some guerrilla-commando-Ninja-SWAT-team-hawk-from-hell attack on the Clinic. And he'll talk Rachel into stomping your house flat."

Everyone laughed, because we all knew why Cassie had birdcages. Her father and mother are both vets. Her mum works for The Gardens, which is this huge zoo and amusement park.

Her dad runs the Wildlife Rehabilitation Clinic in the barn on their family farm. The Clinic takes in wild animals that are sick or hurt and cares for them.

The cages Cassie had to get home to clean were filled with sparrows with broken wings and eagles who'd been shot and seagulls who'd got tangled in rubbish.

Cassie is our expert on animals. She also gets us access to animals to morph. She's a gentle person. She can also morph better than any of us.

Everyone stood up and started to go.

"You coming, Tobias?" Jake asked me.

17

<No, not right away. I think I'll fly around. It's a nice night.>

"Cool," he said. "I'll put some food up in your attic for you in case you get home late. I don't want anything getting at it, though. Can you open one of those Rubbermaid things?"

I saw the way the others kind of looked away when Jake mentioned the attic. They feel sorry for me.

<I can get it open,> I said. <Just be careful. You know — Tom.>

Tom is Jake's big brother. Tom is one of *them*.

Everyone said good night. I saw Cassie and Jake touch their hands together in a way that could almost have been accidental. Then they were all gone. All but me and Rachel.

"I don't like thinking of you living in that cold attic," Rachel said.

<I'm OK,> I said. I wondered if I should tell her what I had seen, the darkness within darkness, the hole in the sky. But the truth was, even I didn't know what it was.

It would just worry her. And she worried about me too much.

<Good night,> I said.

"Yeah. Take care of yourself, Tobias."

I flew out through her window into the night. Rachel's sad eyes seemed to follow me. I hated the way they all felt sorry for me. All they could see was that I was not what I used to be. All they saw was that I had no home.

But they didn't really understand. I hadn't had a real home since my parents died. I was used to being alone.

And I had the sky.

Chapter 4

The next day I decided to go back to where I had seen — or not seen — the big thing in the sky.

I had a feeling about it. A bad feeling.

I flew up over the same area, rising as high as I could on the thermals.

Hawks are not quite as good at soaring high as eagles or some buzzards are. (Man, you should see the way a turkey buzzard can work those thermals! Awesome.) And actually, the red-tail hawk in my head would be just as happy perched patiently on the branch of a tree, waiting to see its next meal go scurrying past.

But I didn't eat like a hawk. I ate food that Jake gave me. I didn't hunt. Although sometimes the urge to hunt was pretty strong.

I could just hear Marco making some smart crack about me eating mice. Or roadkill.

When you're in a morph, it's hard to resist the animal's instincts. Jake found that out when he became a lizard. He gulped down a live spider before he got control of the lizard's instincts.

I hadn't done that. Yet. I was afraid if I did it once, I'd never be able to stop.

I soared high above the city, over the area I'd been through the day before. But nothing. Nothing moved in the air above me.

Then it occurred to me: whatever it was, maybe it only happened at certain times of day. It had been almost sunset when I'd felt its presence last.

I decided to come back around sunset. Which meant I had the whole day ahead of me with nothing special to do. This did not make me happy. See, the fact is, a hawk spends almost all its time hunting food.

As for me, Tobias, when I hadn't been in school, I used to spend most of my free time watching TV, hanging out at the mall, doing homework, reading . . . all things it was difficult for me to do, now.

I missed school. Even though I had constantly been picked on by bullies. I didn't really miss my

21

home, though. See, when my parents died, there was no one who really wanted me. I ended up getting shunted back and forth between an uncle here and an aunt across the country.

Neither of them really cared about me. I don't think they even missed me. I had arranged for Jake to leave a message with my uncle. We told him I had gone to stay with my aunt. Each of them, my uncle and my aunt, thought I was staying with the other.

I had no idea how long that trick would hold up before one of them figured out I wasn't really in either place.

I guess when they realize it they'll call the cops and report me as a runaway. Or maybe they won't even bother.

So. What was I going to do with my day? I'd been floating up here in the high air, just below the clouds, for a couple of hours. It was time to give it up and try again another time.

I tilted my wings and adjusted my tail, turning towards Rachel's house. Maybe she would be hanging around the house, bored.

Then it happened.

Two kilometres or more above me, the ripple passed through the air. An emptiness, a hole where no hole could be.

I reacted instantly. I had to get closer.

I flapped till my chest and shoulders were

sore. But it was moving too fast, and it was too high.

It pulled away from me, a wave of air, a slight rippling of the fabric of the sky. It was moving in a different direction, though. This time it was moving *towards* the mountains.

Then . . . a flight of geese on the move in a tight V-formation.

There were maybe a dozen of the big, determined geese, moving along at an amazing rate, powering their way through the air like they always do. Geese always seem to be on a mission. Like, "Get out of our way, we're geese and we're coming through."

The geese were aimed straight for the disturbance.

Suddenly, the lead goose folded like it had been hit by a truck. Its wings collapsed. But it did not fall.

The crippled goose slid through the air. It slid horizontally, rolling and flopping like it was passing over the top of a racing train.

Most of the other geese suffered the same fate. One or two peeled away in time, but geese are not real agile.

The invisible wave smacked into the flight, and the geese were crushed. They were rolling and sliding along some unseen but solid surface.

And everywhere the geese hit, I could catch

23

little glimpses of steel-grey metal.

The wave passed by. The geese fell in its wake, dead or crippled.

It flew on, unconcerned. But then, why should the Yeerks care about a handful of geese?

And that's what they were, I was certain. Yeerks.

What I had seen, or not quite seen, was a Yeerk ship.

Chapter 5

"It figures," Marco said thoughtfully. "The Yeerks would have to have some kind of cloaking ability. Like our 'stealth' technology, only much better."

We are all in Cassie's barn. Her dad was away for the afternoon. And it's one of the few places where I can go and not look out of place.

It's a regular old-fashioned barn, but with rows of clean cages and fluorescent lights. There are partitions keeping the birds away from the horses, and more partitions keeping the raccoons and opossums and the occasional coyote away from the skittish horses. The floor of the barn is usually strewn with hoses and buckets and scattered hay. There are charts on each cage showing the condition of the animal and what treatment it's getting.

It's usually a pretty noisy place, what with various birds chirping or cooing, horses snuffling, and raccoons fussing with their food.

I looked over a little nervously at a pair of wolves, one male, one female. One had been shot. The other had eaten poison left out by a farmer. The wolves were new in the area. Animal experts had brought some back to live wild in the nearby forest.

Wolves make hawks a little edgy.

"We were always able to see Yeerk ships," Rachel pointed out. "We saw the Bug fighters and the Blade ship." She was leaning against a cage that housed an injured mourning dove. The dove was watching me suspiciously.

"Yeah, but every Yeerk ship we've ever dealt with has been either on the ground or about to land," Jake said. "Maybe the cloaking ability doesn't work when they get close to land. But if you think about it, Marco is right. They would have to be able to avoid being picked up by radar. Maybe they also have the ability to avoid being seen."

<It was a Yeerk ship,> I said flatly.

"How can you be so sure?" Cassie asked. She was working as we talked, cleaning an empty cage with a brush and a bucket of sudsy water.

<It just was,> I said stubbornly. <I . . . I just got this feeling from it. Also, it seemed huge. Far bigger than even the biggest jet. This was huge. More like a real ship, you know, like an ocean liner.>

"The question is, what do we do about it?" Jake asked. Of course, I knew he'd already made up his mind to do *something*. But Jake doesn't like to act like the one in charge, even though that's how I think of him. He lets everyone have their say first.

<I want to find out what it's doing,> I said. <The first time, I had the feeling it was heading away from the mountains. The second time, it was doing just the opposite. It was flying too low to make it *over* the mountains. So I'm guessing it was doing something *in* the mountains.>

Rachel nodded. "That makes sense."

Marco rolled his eyes. "The mountains? Have you suburb-dwellers ever been to the mountains? We're talking about a large area. No matter how big this ship is, it could hide in a thousand places in the mountains."

"Then we'd better start looking right away," Rachel said brightly.

Jake looked at Cassie. "Cass? What do you think?"

Cassie shrugged. "I halfway feel like we've done enough. You know? We attacked the Yeerk pool. We barely got out alive. We infiltrated Chapman's house and Rachel was captured. Again, we barely got out alive. I guess the question is, how many risks are we going to take? How many more times are we going to barely escape?"

I could see that Marco was surprised. Suddenly it sounded like Cassie was on his side. "Exactly! Exactly! Just what I've been saying. Why is it our job to get killed?"

But then Cassie went and blew it all for him.

"I mean, as far as I'm concerned, I can't just do *nothing* while people are enslaved by the Yeerks," Cassie said. "Maybe it's just me . . ." She shrugged. "The thing is, I have these powers." She shrugged again. "I can't just sit and do nothing."

"Look, these aren't people we know," Marco argued. "They aren't my friends. Or my family." He shot a guilty look at Jake. "And we did everything we could for Tom. So why should I get killed for strangers? We can't stay lucky forever. Don't you people understand that? Sooner or later, we'll slip up. Sooner or later we'll be standing around here crying because Jake or Rachel or Cassie or Tobias is gone."

"You know something?" Rachel exploded. "I'm tired of trying to talk you into this, Marco. You want out? Fine, you're OUT!"

"Hey, Rachel, you're not just doing this to

help save the human race," Marco yelled back. "You get off on the danger. That's why you went with Tobias to free that bird. That wasn't about saving the world. That was about rescuing some stupid bird."

Marco realized he'd gone too far. He fell silent. The others all looked guiltily at me. Rachel shot Marco a look of pure anger.

<As of right now,> I said, <as of today, only one of us has been hurt. Me. But I'm not going to give up. I'm not anyone's leader. But what I am going to do is go to the mountains tomorrow morning. What the rest of you do is your business.>

"I'll be with you," Rachel said instantly.

Cassie nodded.

Jake made a wry smile. "You say you're not a leader, but I'll go with you."

Marco shook his head. "No," he said.

"Your choice," Rachel said.

"That's not what I meant," Marco said angrily. "I meant no, not in the morning. Tomorrow's a school day. If all of us skip school on the same day and later there's some trouble with the Yeerks, don't you think Chapman might put two and two together?"

Jake raised an eyebrow. "Marco's right. After school." He looked at the others and nodded.

It bothered me that Marco was right. But he

29

was. Marco might be a pain in the neck. But he's a very smart guy.

It worried me a little. It made me wonder. Was he right about other things as well?

How many risks could we take before we lost? How long till the five of us were four? Or two?

Or none?

Chapter 6

Jake had a peregrine falcon morph that we'd used before. Marco and Cassie had also morphed ospreys. Rachel had been a bald eagle. So we all should have been able to fly up to the mountains.

But there are millions of bird-watchers in this country. They're very cool people because they never hurt a bird. They don't hunt. They just get pleasure out of watching birds fly or nest.

Bird-watchers would think it was very, very weird if they saw a red-tail hawk, a bald eagle, a falcon, and two ospreys all flying together as if they were on a mission.

And some of those gentle bird-watchers might be not-so-gentle Controllers.

"Bird-watchers!" Marco snorted as he tramped over the carpet of pine needles deeper into the woods. "We could fly, but no. No, we have to walk. Thirty kilometres, probably!"

Cassie's farm has a lot of open grass areas, and it borders on a national forest. The national forest goes on forever. It stretches from the edge of town all the way up into the mountains. It's all pines and oaks and elms and birches. Wilderness, really. Thousands of hectares of it.

"Oh, come on, Marco," Cassie chided gently. "It's an opportunity to try out a new morph!"

"Yeah," Jake chided. "Instead of being home doing maths homework, you get to turn into a wolf. Are you really going to tell me you'd rather be doing equations?"

"Let's see," Marco considered. "Maths? Or becoming a wolf and going off to find aliens? Maybe I should ask the school counsellor what she thinks. It's such a common problem. I'm sure she'd have some good advice."

Since it wasn't a good idea for us all to travel to the mountains as birds, the others needed a morph that could travel far and fast through woods. And there were the two injured wolves in Cassie's barn . . .

Jake stopped, looked around, and announced, "This is good." We were a few hundred metres into the woods. I came to rest on a low branch of a huge oak tree. The hawk in me took note of a squirrel a few branches up. He started chittering and shrieking his little squirrel warning. Danger! Danger!

Hawk! Hawk!

I gave him a look. He twitched, stuck the acorn he was holding into his cheek, and took off at full speed.

"What I don't get is why I have to be a girl wolf," Marco grumbled.

"We had one male and one female," Cassie explained for the tenth time. "If two of us morphed into the male, we'd have two males. Two male wolves might decide they had to fight for dominance."

"I could control it," Marco said.

"Marco, you and Jake *already* fight for dominance, and you're just ordinary guys," Rachel pointed out.

"She's right," Cassie said sadly. "I'm afraid your primitive male behaviour might slow us down."

"Hey, when I morphed into a gorilla, I handled that gorilla brain OK, didn't I?" Marco demanded.

"Sure, Marco," Rachel said. She batted her eyes. "But that was different. You and the gorilla were already so much alike."

Cassie and Rachel gave each other discreet high-fives.

"Hugely funny," Marco said.

"We flipped a coin, fair and square," Jake said. "I got to be the male. You're one of the females. Get over it."

"Let me see that coin again," Marco said suspiciously.

Jake just smiled. "Let's just do this. Cassie, you want to go first, to see what it's like?"

We had learned from hard experience that morphing can be extremely disturbing. Jake had morphed into a lizard and been almost overpowered by the animal's fearful brain. The same had happened to Rachel when she'd morphed a shrew. She still had nightmares about the shrew experience — its fear and, worse, its hunger for bugs and rotting flesh.

On the other hand, Jake had morphed into a flea, and according to him it was kind of a big nothing. Like being trapped inside a very old, very bad video game where you could barely see anything. The flea brain had been too simple to make trouble.

"Okay. I'll let you know." Cassie closed her eyes and concentrated. Then she opened them again. "Wait. Let me get down to my morph suit first. I don't want to get tangled up in my clothes."

She removed everything but a leotard, kicked

off her shoes, and stood barefoot on the pine needles.

The first change was her hair. It went from very short black to shaggy silver in just a few seconds. It travelled down from her head, down her neck, over her shoulders, around her neck. Long, shaggy fur.

Then her nose bulged out.

I shuddered. You never really get used to seeing people morph. It is something straight out of a nightmare. Even though Cassie seems to have some kind of talent for it. She's never quite as gross as the others. I guess it's because she's so close to so many animals. Maybe she just has a special feel for them.

Still, as the wolf snout began to push out from her face, it was not a pleasant sight.

Her ears grew furry and pointed. Then they slid straight up the side of her head till they almost touched on top.

Her eyes went from brown-black to golden brown.

All over her body, the fur replaced the bright pinks and greens of her leotard. A tail suddenly shot out from behind. I could hear the grinding of her bones as they rearranged. Her upper arms shortened. Her lower arms grew longer. Fingers shrivelled and disappeared, leaving behind only stubby black nails.

There was a sickening crunch as her knees changed direction. Her legs shrank and thinned and grew fur.

Suddenly she fell forward, no longer able to stand erect.

It had taken about two minutes.

Cassie was now a wolf.

"How is it?" Jake asked.

Cassie jerked suddenly at the sound of his voice and spun around to face him. She bared her teeth and snarled a warning that would have made a Taxxon back up.

She had very impressive teeth.

"Let's all stand really still," Jake said.

"Good idea," Marco agreed. "Really, really still. Because those are really, really big teeth."

Everyone stood motionless. They had all been through similar experiences. We knew what was happening. Inside the wolf's head, Cassie was fighting to gain control of the wolf's wild instincts.

<Sorry,> she thought-spoke at last. <I have it now.>

"Are you sure?" Rachel asked warily.

<Yes, it's fine. I'm fine. In fact . . . it's really kind of wonderful! The sense of hearing. Wow! And my nose. Whoa, that's incredible. I've never morphed an animal with such a strong sense of smell.>

"Then I'm extra glad I put on deodorant," Marco joked.

<Who had bacon for breakfast?> Cassie turned her wolf head this way and that. <Rachel? Bacon? I thought you were going to go vegetarian!>

Marco laughed at the guilty look on Rachel's face. "Oooh, busted by Cassie the wonder-nose."

"Let's get busy," Jake said. "The two-hour clock is now running. Tick-tock."

One by one they each stole a glance at me. I'm the handy reminder of what happens if you stay in a morph for too long.

Chapter 7

I was jealous.

I mean, OK, if you ever have to be stuck as an animal, I think being a hawk is the coolest choice of all.

But still, I was jealous. My friends were really enjoying being wolves. I guess it was a strange experience for them.

I flew above the forest, skimming the tree-tops, while down below they ran. They moved so fast it wasn't always easy for me to keep up. Not that their actual speed was so great. It's just that they never stopped. Never rested. They just moved at a constant thirty kilometres an hour or so. Over fallen logs. Between trees. Under bushes. Nothing even slowed them down.

Well, actually, that's not completely true. Two things slowed them down a little.

One was Jake. He was the dominant male. In wolf packs that's called an "alpha." So he had a special wolf job to perform.

<Jake, just how many more times are you going to pee?> Rachel demanded after his fifth stop.

<I . . . I don't know. I kind of have to do it a lot,> he admitted.

<Why? Did you drink too much soda before we left?>

<I don't know,> he admitted. <I just keep getting this urge to pee.>

<You're scent marking,> Cassie explained. <You're marking out a territory.>

<I am?>

<Yes, you are. It's normal. For a dominant wolf. At least that's what my wolf book said. Although it's a little gross for the rest of us to have to watch.>

The other thing that slowed them down was when they stopped once and started to howl. It was Jake who started it. It caught everyone by surprise. Including Jake himself.

"OWWW-OOOOOOO-yow-yow-OOOOOO."

<What the — > Marco started to say, but then he was doing it, too. "Yow-yow-OOWWOOOOO!"

Cassie and Rachel weren't far behind.

"OOOOO-yowww-OWW-OOOOOOO!"

I heard the yowling, of course, so I took a quick turn around a tree and headed back to them. <What are you people doing?> I demanded. <We're in a hurry here. You guys can only stay in morph for two hours. Why are you wasting time howling?>

<I don't know,> Jake admitted sheepishly. <I just suddenly felt like it would be a good idea.>

<Once he started I . . . I kind of felt like I should join in,> Rachel said.

<I think it's a way to warn all the other wolves that we're here, so we don't run into any other packs and get in fights,> Cassie suggested. Which sounded perfectly reasonable. Until you saw that "Cassie" had her head tilted back and her snout pointed at the sky and was yodelling like an idiot.

I flapped my wings and broke out from under the trees. The city and the suburbs were far behind me now. We had travelled pretty far in an hour's time. It was about the same time of day as my second sighting of the invisible ship. The time when it had been heading towards the mountains.

I swooped back down into the trees. <You guys keep moving. I'm going up top to look around.>

<Be careful,> Rachel said.

I banked left around a tree, then flapped my way back up into the sun. I climbed hard and fast, using a lot of energy. The exercise helped distract me. It's hard feeling sorry for yourself when you're working out big time.

After a while I was able to catch a nice thermal and get some easy altitude. I could still see the little wolf pack, moving like it had a single mind, flowing around the trees, swift and sure.

I tried to imagine what it must be like to be a wolf. The amazing sense of smell. The incredible hearing. All that confident power, those ripping teeth, the cool intelligence.

Maybe later I would ask Jake or Rachel about it.

Then you could ask them what it was like to be human. Maybe they can tell me about that, too, I thought bitterly.

Stop it, Tobias, I ordered myself. *Stop it.*

I guess I felt that if I ever started to feel really sorry for myself, I might never stop.

I kept a sharp eye out on the sky above, but it was probably still too early for the ship to come. If it even came. There was no reason to think it kept some kind of schedule.

Then, down below, I saw something that caught my attention. There was a convoy of trucks and Jeeps moving along a narrow, snaking dirt road. Maybe five vehicles. They had the

41

markings of the Park Service. But they seemed to be in a big hurry.

They drove to a lake that I had just glimpsed up ahead. By the shore of the lake, they pulled off the road. Then, to my surprise, several dozen uniformed men jumped from the trucks and began to fan out through the woods.

They were carrying guns. But not rifles or even pistols. I could see them clearly. They were carrying automatic weapons.

Suddenly, movement in the sky! What the —

To my left I spotted a pair of helicopters. They zipped just metres above the trees. They began to circle the lake. These also had Park Service markings.

This is all wrong, I told myself. *These guys don't act or move like Park Rangers. These guys move like an army.*

And as I watched, half a dozen of the armed men surrounded a small patch of bright yellow. It was a tent.

Two people — they looked like college types — were cooking over a little fire outside the tent.

I could see the expressions of total amazement and fear when they suddenly realized they were surrounded by six men with automatic weapons.

The two campers were marched back to the

nearest truck and driven away at high speed.

I don't know what story the two campers were told. Maybe the Park Rangers told them there was a dangerous fugitive in the area. Or maybe they said there was a forest fire. I don't know. I just know those two campers were out of there before they knew what hit them.

The two choppers circled the lake. Then they landed in a small clearing at the far side of the lake at the same time.

It was more than a kilometre away. Far, even for my hawk's eyes, in the slanting light of afternoon. But I could still see what came out of those helicopters.

Out they leaped, one after another.

Two metres tall. The most dangerous-looking creatures you'll ever want to see. Long, razor-sharp blades raked forward from their snake heads. More blades at their elbows, wrists, and knees. Feet like Tyrannosaurus rex.

The shock troops of the Yeerks.

Hork-Bajir warriors.

43

Chapter 8

<Hork-Bajir!>

The first time I'd seen them was that night at the construction site. I was still fully human then. It was while Visser Three was taunting the fallen Andalite. The five of us had been cowering behind a low wall. A Hork-Bajir had been within a few metres of us.

The Andalite told us they had once been a good people, the Hork-Bajir. That despite their fearsome appearance, they were a gentle race.

But the Hork-Bajir were all Controllers now. They all carried the Yeerk slug in their brains. And they were no longer gentle.

I made a sharp turn back. I had to warn the

others. I passed over a group of the Park Rangers, and swooped low enough to read one man's watch. My friends had been in morph for more than an hour.

Great. Low on time, and the Hork-Bajir are here.

I soon spotted the wolf pack, still trotting along resolutely, never tiring. Pausing only for Jake to pee.

I dived towards them. Just over their heads I pulled up suddenly.

"Yowl! Yip! Rrawr!"

They yelped and scampered around. Jake bared his fangs at me.

I came to rest on a decayed log.

Instantly, as if on command, the others started fanning out around me, encircling me. The five of them were acting like a wolf pack surrounding prey. In their own way they kind of reminded me of Hork-Bajir.

<Hey, it's just me, relax,> I said.

No answer. Jake snarled a brief command at one of the others.

Wait a minute. *Five?* Five wolves?

Jake, who wasn't really Jake, leaped at me.

Whoa!

Wolves don't usually hurt humans, but they will definitely eat a bird when they're hungry enough. And one thing you don't ever want to see

45

is a hungry wolf, yellowed fangs bared, gold-brown eyes glaring, fur bristling, coming at you.

I flapped my wings hard.

The big male wolf went shooting past. Barely. But the rest were all around me!

I flapped again and got airborne, but just a few centimetres. I was skimming wildly over the pine-needle carpet, flapping for all I was worth, with five determined wolves hot on my tail.

SWOOOOM! I caught the tiniest headwind, but it was all I needed.

I was up! Up and out of there, while the wolves yowled and snapped their powerful jaws in frustration below me.

Ten minutes later I found a second wolf pack. This time I counted. *Four* wolves.

Still, I was cautious. <Is that you guys?>

<Who else would it be?> Marco asked.

<Don't ask,> I said. <Look, we have trouble.> I flapped down to a low branch and rested my wings. I was still a little shaken up from my close call with the wrong wolves.

<There's a lake just a little way ahead. It's crawling with Park Rangers who aren't really Park Rangers.>

<Yeah, I thought I smelled some water. And humans,> Cassie said.

<How do you know they aren't real Park Rangers?> Jake asked.

46

<Because real Park Rangers don't carry machine guns,> I said. <Plus, they don't hang around with Hork-Bajir.>

<Hork-Bajir?> Cassie asked shakily. <You're sure?>

<Oh yeah,> I said. <It's kind of hard to confuse them with anything else. The Park Rangers are clearing out the area around the lake. They hustled some campers out of there real fast. At gunpoint.>

<Hork-Bajir,> Marco said with some distaste. <I really don't like those guys.>

Rachel asked, <This lake, it's in the same direction your big invisible ship was moving?>

<It's in a perfectly straight line,> I said. <Whatever that ship was, I'd bet anything it was heading for that lake.>

<And judging by the way you say these Park-Ranger Controllers and Hork-Bajir are acting, it's on its way again,> Marco said thoughtfully.

<I'll tell you one thing,> I said. <These guys all looked like they'd done this many times before. You know what I mean? Like this was a real common routine. They had it down.>

<We don't have a lot of time left in morph,> Jake said. <But it would be a shame to miss the chance to find out what this is all about.>

<I say go for it,> Rachel said.

<You *always* say go for it,> Marco muttered.

47

<If just once you would say, 'Hey, let's *not* do this,' it would make me so happy.>

<You have about forty minutes left,> I told them. <The lake is about five minutes away.>

<Okay. Let's go. But in and out fast,> Jake warned. <Just enough to see what's going on.> They took off, with Jake in the lead. <Remember, just act like wolves.>

<Yeah, so if anyone sees the Three Little Pigs, don't forget to huff and puff,> Marco said.

I went airborne again, but this time I stayed close by.

<Park Rangers just ahead,> I said.

<Yeah, I can definitely smell them now,> Rachel replied. <And hear them, too.>

<Okay, look, wolves would try to steer clear of humans,> Cassie advised. <So a little slinking would be perfectly normal.>

They moved in a cautious circle around the fake Park Rangers. But I could see that the Rangers had spotted them. They tensed up, then relaxed when they saw it was just a wolf pack minding its own business.

I decided to get some altitude. Unfortunately, since there were no convenient thermals, I had to flap my way up. I was a few thousand metres high, able to see my friends and the lake, when I felt its presence again.

I looked up.

The invisible wave. The slight ripple in the fabric of the sky. It was there. It was moving slowly overhead. Even more slowly than before.

And then, as I watched, it was invisible no more.

Chapter 9

<Don't act suspicious or freak,> I called down to the others. <But look up.>

<Oh my God,> Rachel gasped.

<It's . . . it's huge!> Cassie cried.

It was huge. But the word huge doesn't really begin to describe it.

Have you ever seen a picture of an oil tanker? Or maybe an aircraft carrier? That's what I mean by huge. Compared to this thing, the biggest jumbo jet ever built was a toy.

It was shaped like a manta ray. There was a bulging, fat portion in the middle, with swooped, curvy wings, one either side. On top of the wings were huge scoops, like air intakes on a fighter jet, but much bigger. You could suck a fleet of buses in through those scoops.

The only windows were in a small bulge at the top. The bridge, I realized. Focusing on it, I could see the shadowy shapes of Taxxons inside.

But mostly that ship was just big. Really big. As in, it blocked out the sun, it was so big.

Suddenly, out from behind the ship, a pair of Bug fighters zipped into view. We had seen them before. They are small, for spaceships. You couldn't park one in your garage, but you could land it on your front lawn. They look like metal cockroaches with two serrated spearlike protrusions pointed forward on either side.

<I have Bug fighters up here,> I called down to the others. <A pair.>

<Who cares about Bug fighters?> Marco asked. <They're nothing compared to that . . . that whale!>

<The Bug fighters are circling the lake. I guess they're looking around for trouble.>

<Try not to look like trouble,> Jake advised dryly.

I did my best to look like a normal, harmless hawk. Doing normal hawk things. But the main ship was unbelievably intimidating. I mean, nothing that big should be floating in the air.

Suddenly one of the Bug fighters shot right

past me, low and slow. I could see in the window. Inside was the usual crew: one Hork-Bajir and one Taxxon.

The Taxxons are the second most common type of Controller. Imagine a very big centipede. Now imagine it even bigger, twice as long as a man. So big around, you couldn't get your arms around it if you wanted to give it a hug.

Not that you'd ever want to give it a hug. Taxxons are gross, disgusting creatures. Unlike the Hork-Bajir, who were enslaved against their will, Taxxons chose to turn their minds over to the Yeerk parasites. They are allies of the Yeerks. I don't know why, and I probably don't want to.

The Bug fighter shot past, not interested in me.

The huge main ship sank slowly down towards the surface of the lake. <Are you guys seeing this? It looks like it's going to land on the lake.>

<Are we seeing it? No. We've totally missed the fact that a spaceship the size of Delaware is hovering in midair.>

Marco, of course.

<It's incredible,> Rachel said. <Incredible.>

<You know, I hate to be a pessimist,> Marco said, <but when I look at that thing I get a bad feeling about our chances. Four hounds and a bird versus a ship the size of Idaho!>

<A minute ago it was just the size of Delaware,> Cassie pointed out mildly.

<What's it doing here? That's what I want to know,> Jake said.

They had reached the shore of the lake and were prowling along, looking like wolves should look. But they were also glancing regularly up at the massive ship. I worried a little that some Controller, human or Hork-Bajir, would notice that they were paying a little too much attention.

<You guys? Watch how you act. The Yeerks will be looking for any animals that act strangely,> I said. <They're on the lookout for Andalites who can morph.>

<He's right,> Marco agreed. <Jake? Start peeing on things again.>

<Very funny,> Jake said.

Then something began to happen. <Hey. Look!>

From the belly of the ship, a pipe began to lower into the water. Then a second pipe, and a third.

<They're like straws,> Cassie said. <They're *drinking*!>

I could hear the sucking sound. Thousands, maybe millions of litres of water being sucked up into the ship.

<That's why it's so big,> Marco said. He laughed. <Well, well, well. What do you know? We have just discovered that the Yeerks have a great big weakness.>

<A weakness?> Rachel demanded. <You can look at that ship and talk about *weakness*?>

But I understood what Marco meant. <It means they need something,> I said.

<Exactly,> Marco said. <Those big scoops on the sides? I think those are for air. That's why they fly so far through the atmosphere when they come down. They're scooping up oxygen. And now they are sucking up water.>

<It's a truck!> Cassie cried. <That whole huge ship is really just a truck!>

<Yeah,> I said. <It carries air and water up to the Yeerk mother ship in orbit. I guess they need Earth to supply them.>

<So. It's not like *Star Trek*, where they can just make their own air and water,> Marco mused. <As long as they are up there in orbit, the Yeerks need the planet to supply them with fresh air and water. Well, well. I think that's the first hopeful sign yet.>

<We're running low on time,> Cassie reminded everyone. <Time to get out of here.>

<Okay, but everyone be cool about it,> Jake advised. <We act like we're just sauntering off to go kill a moose — or whatever it is wolves saunter off to do.>

They drifted back from the shore of the lake. I stayed behind. I no longer have a time limit to worry about.

The Yeerk ship was creating a warm updraft, so I spread my wings wide and rode it up. The two Bug fighters were still circling low and slow. On the shore all around the lake, the bogus Park Rangers and the few Hork-Bajir kept up their patrols.

Then I saw her.

I know to human eyes, every hawk looks pretty much alike. But I knew right away it was her — the hawk I had freed from the car dealer.

She, too, was riding the thermal, a thousand metres higher than me. Without even really thinking about it, I adjusted the angle of my wings and soared up towards her.

She saw me, I was sure of that. Hawks don't miss much of what goes on around them. She knew I was coming towards her, and she waited.

It wasn't like we were friends. Hawks don't know what "friend" means. And she certainly did not feel any gratitude towards me for saving her from captivity. Hawks don't have that sort of emotion, either. In fact, in her mind there may have been no connection between me and her freedom.

Still, I soared up to her. I don't know why. I really don't. All we shared was the same outer body. We both had wings. We both had talons. We both had feathers.

Suddenly I was afraid. I was afraid of her. And

it was insane, because there I was, floating above an alien spaceship so big it could have been turned into a shopping mall.

But it was the hawk that frightened me.

Or maybe not the hawk herself. Maybe it was the feeling I had, rising up to meet her in the sky.

The feeling of recognition. The feeling of going home. The feeling that I belonged with her.

It hit me in a wave of disgust and horror.

No. NO!

I was Tobias. A human. A human being, not a bird!

I banked sharply away from her.

I was *human*. I was a boy named Tobias. A boy with blond hair that was always a mess. A boy with human friends. Human interests.

But part of me kept saying, "It's a lie. It's a lie. You are now the hawk. The hawk is you. And Tobias is dead."

I plummeted towards the ground. I folded my wings back and welcomed the sheer speed. Faster! Faster!

Then, with eyes that Tobias never had, I saw the wolf pack below. And I saw the danger before them.

Chapter 10

My four friends stood stock still. Staring with deadly focus at five other wolves.

The two packs had run into each other. Between them lay a dead rabbit. It was the other pack's kill. My friends had stumbled into them. Now the two alpha males were locked in a deadly dominance battle.

One of those alpha males was Jake.

The other was an actual wolf.

Jake had human intelligence on his side. But if it came to a fight, the other wolf had more experience. He hadn't got to be the head wolf in his pack by losing fights.

I would have laughed if I could. It was ridiculous! But at least it took my mind off the female hawk. Off the feeling that drew me to her, that called out to me, even while Yeerk ships zipped in a deadly dance through the air.

Then it hit me with a shock: the time! They'd been low on time when they'd left the shore and started back. How much time had elapsed?

I swooped down low. <What are you guys doing?> I demanded.

<Shut up, Tobias,> Jake snapped tersely. <We're in a situation here.>

<Yeah, I can see that. Back away from them.>

<I can't. If I back off, I lose.>

<Lose *what*?> I yelled. <You're not a wolf. He's a wolf. Let him be *boss* wolf. You guys are way low on time!>

<It's not that simple,> Cassie said. <If Jake looks weak, the other alpha may attack. We screwed up. We're in their territory. And they think we're trying to steal their kill.>

Suddenly the other big male snarled and took a step forward. Instantly Jake bared his teeth still further and stood his ground.

The dead rabbit lay between them, only a few metres from the vicious teeth on either side.

<This fight's over the rabbit, right?> I said.

No answer. Everyone was so tense they were quivering. At any second this would explode into all-out gang warfare of the wolf variety.

I knew what I should do. But it went against every instinct in the hawk's brain.

And Tobias the human wasn't exactly thrilled, either.

I flapped up to gain a little height. I would need the speed. Then I locked my eyes on that rabbit and prayed that I was as fast as I thought I was.

<Oh, maaaaaan!>

Down I shot. My talons came forward.

"Tseeeeer!" I screamed.

Zoom!

A wolf on each side.

A dead rabbit.

Thwack! My talons hit the dead animal and snatched at the fur.

I flapped once, twice. The rabbit came off the ground.

The big wolf lunged. I could feel his teeth rake my tail.

I flapped for all I was worth, scooting along the ground, half-carrying, half-dragging the dead rabbit, with the big wolf racing just centimetres behind me.

<Tobias!> Rachel cried.

<Get out of here!> I yelled. <I have to drop this thing. It's too heavy!>

Fortunately, when he isn't being an idiot wolf,

59

Jake is quick and decisive. <Let's go while we can!>

I dropped the rabbit just as the wolf caught up to me.

SNAP!

Jaws that could kill a moose scissored the air a centimetre from me. I'm telling you, he was close enough for me to count his molars.

I felt the tiniest bit of a breeze. It was enough. I opened my wings and let the breeze lift me up and away.

<Oh, that was really not fun,> I said.

<Are you OK?>

<I think I lost some tail feathers,> I said. Tail feathers grow back.

I caught up with the others. They were moving as fast as wolves can move. Time was running short. I didn't know exactly how much time. It was one of the continuing problems of morphing. Even if you *could* wear a watch, you wouldn't want to. A wolf or a hawk with a watch looks slightly suspicious.

<I'll see if I can get a time reading,> I said. I was tired. Very tired, after the long flight here and not one but two close calls involving wolves. The hawk in me just wanted to find a nice branch with a view of an open field and take a rest. But I knew I couldn't.

I gained a little altitude, not too much. Just

enough to spot one of the Park Service trucks.
The Controllers were off somewhere, but there
was a clock in the dashboard.

I stared at the number in disbelief.

It had to be wrong! It had to be!

Chapter 11

I wasn't tired any more.

At top speed, I raced back to my friends. I felt sick. I felt like my heart was going to burst.

They had missed the deadline! It was too late. Too late, and they would all be trapped. Like me. Forever.

<MORPH!> I screamed as I closed in on them.

Thought-speak is like regular speech. It gets harder to hear the farther away you are.

<Morph back! Now!> Maybe the clock in the truck was off. Maybe five minutes one way or the other wouldn't matter.

There! I saw them. Four wolves moving relentlessly towards the distant city.

<Morph! Now!> I screamed as I shot like a bullet over their heads.

<How much time do we have?!> Marco demanded.

<None.>

That got them going. I landed, exhausted, on a branch.

Cassie was the first to begin the change. Her fur grew short. Her snout flattened into a nose. Long, human legs swelled and burst from the thin dog legs.

Her tail sucked back in and disappeared. She was already more than half human by the time the first changes began to appear on the others.

<Come on, hurry,> I urged them.

<What time is it?> Jake demanded.

<You have about two minutes,> I said. It was a lie. According to the clock, they were already seven minutes too late.

Too late.

And yet Cassie was continuing to emerge from her wolf body. Skin was replacing fur. Her leotard covered her legs.

But the others were not so lucky.

<*Ahhhh!*> I heard Rachel cry in my mind. Her morph was going all wrong. Her human hands appeared at the end of her wolf legs. But nothing else seemed to be changing.

I looked, horrified, at Marco. His normal head

63

emerged with startling suddenness from his wolf body. But the rest of him had not changed. He looked down at himself and cried out in terror. "Helowl. Yipmeahhh!" It was an awful sound, half human, half wolf.

This was worse than I had feared. I figured they could be trapped as wolves, like I had been trapped as a hawk. But they were emerging as half-human freaks of nature.

They were living nightmares.

Cassie ran from one to the next. "Come on, Jake, concentrate! Focus! Rachel, bear down, girl. Picture yourself human. See yourself like you're looking in the mirror. Fight the fear, Marco!"

I saw Marco roll his human eyes up and stare at me. His gaze locked on me. It was like he hated me. Or feared me. Both, maybe.

I didn't move. If Marco needed me to concentrate, that was fine.

But it sent a shiver of disgust through me. I suddenly saw myself as they all must see me: as something frightening. A freak. An accident. A sickening, pitiable creature.

Slowly, slowly, Marco began to emerge. Slowly, slowly, the human body appeared.

Rachel, too, and Jake. They were winning their battle.

"That's it, Jake," Cassie urged. She held his hand tight between both of hers. "Come back to me, Jake. Come all the way back."

I watched Rachel. She still had a small, shrinking tail. Her mouth still protruded. Her blonde hair was still more like grey fur. But she was going to make it. The clock must have been fast. A matter of five minutes one way or the other had determined their fates.

I was glad they had made it. They were all human again.

"We did it," Jake gasped weakly. He lay on his back on the pine needles. "We made it."

"That was close," Rachel said. "That was way too close. It was so hard. It was like trying to climb up out of a pool of molasses."

"I'm human again," Marco muttered. "Human! Toes. Hands. Arms and shoulders." He checked himself all over.

"Ha ha! That was *close*!" Cassie exulted. She gave Jake a hug. Then I guess she felt self-conscious, because she ran over and hugged Rachel and Marco.

They were all laughing, all giggling with relief.

"We're OK," Jake sighed.

I was happy for them. Really I was. But suddenly I didn't want to be there.

Suddenly I desperately didn't want to be

there. I felt an awful, gaping black hole open up all around me. I was sick. Sick with the feeling of being trapped.

Trapped.

Forever!

I looked at my talons. They would never be feet again.

I looked at my wing. It would never be an arm. It would never again end in a hand. I would never touch. I would never touch anything . . . any*one* . . . again.

I dropped from the branch and opened my wings.

"Tobias!" Jake shouted after me.

But I couldn't stay. I flapped like a demon, no longer caring that I was tired. I had to fly. I had to get away.

"Tobias, no! Come back!" Rachel cried.

I caught a blessed breeze and soared up and away, my own silent, voiceless scream echoing in my head.

Chapter 12

It was late when I returned to what was now my home.

After I was first trapped in my hawk body, Jake had removed an outside panel that led into the attic of his house. I flew in through the opening. It was a typical attic. There were some dusty old cardboard boxes full of Jake and Tom's old baby clothes. There were open boxes of Christmas lights and decorations. There was a chest of drawers with a top that had been scarred by something or other.

Jake had opened one of the drawers in the chest and packed it with an old blanket.

It was nice of him to do that. Jake has always

67

been a decent guy. In the old days he used to protect me from the punks at school who liked to beat me up.

The old days. When I still went to school. How long ago had it been? A few weeks? A month? Not even.

There was a rubber dish in a corner where no one was likely to see it. I was hungry. I clutched the dish with my left talon and pried the lid off with my hooked beak.

Meat and potatoes and green beans. The meat was hamburger. I don't know how he arranged to get the food. His mum probably thought he was sneaking scraps to his dog, Homer.

I hadn't told him yet, but I couldn't eat the vegetables or the potatoes. My system couldn't deal with much except meat. I . . . the hawk . . . was a predator. In the wild, hawks live on rat and squirrel and rabbit.

I ate some of the hamburger. It was cold. It was dead. It made me feel bad to be eating it, but it filled me up.

But it wasn't dead meat that I wanted. I wanted *live* meat. I wanted living, breathing, scurrying prey. I wanted to swoop down on it and grab it with my razor talons and tear into it.

That's what I wanted. What the hawk wanted. And when it came to food, it was hard to deny the hawk brain in my head. The hunger I felt was the hunger of the hawk.

I flopped and hopped up into my drawer. But it was soft. And what my hawk body wanted was not the warmth and comfort of the blanket.

Hawks make nests of sticks. Hawks spend their nights on a friendly branch, feeling the breeze, hearing the nervous chittering of prey, watching the owls hunt.

I hopped up out of the drawer. I couldn't stay there. I was so tired I was past being able to rest. I was restless.

I flew back out into the night. Hawks are not usually nocturnal. The night belongs to other hunters. But I wasn't ready to rest.

I flew aimlessly for a while, but I knew in my heart where I was going.

Rachel's bedroom light was still on. I fluttered down and landed on a birdhouse she had deliberately nailed out there for me to land on when I came over.

I rustled my wing softly against the glass. I scratched with one talon. <Rachel?>

A moment later the window slid up. She was there, wearing a bathrobe and fuzzy slippers.

"Hi," she said. "I was worried about you!"

<Why?> I asked. But I knew the answer.

"We weren't very sensitive this afternoon," she said. She spoke in a whisper. We couldn't let

69

her mother or one of her little sisters overhear her having a one-sided conversation with no one.

<Don't be silly,> I said. <You guys barely escaped being . . . you know.>

"Come inside. I have my bedroom door locked."

I hopped in through the window and fluttered over to her dresser.

Suddenly I realized something was behind me. I turned my head around. It was a mirror. I was looking at myself.

I had a reddish tail of long straight feathers. The rest of my back was mottled dark brown. I had big shoulders that looked kind of hunched, like I was a rugby player ready for the scrum. My head was streamlined. My brown eyes were fierce as I stared over the deadly sharp weapon of my beak.

I turned my head forward, looking away from my reflection. <I don't know what's happening to me, Rachel.>

"What do you mean, Tobias?"

I wish I could have smiled. She looked so worried. I wish I could have smiled, just a little, to make her feel better.

<Rachel. I think I'm losing myself.>

"Wh — What . . . How do you mean?" she asked. She bit her lip and tried not to let me see. But of course, hawk eyes miss nothing.

<Today the hawk we freed . . . she was there. At the lake. I wanted to go with her. I felt like I belonged with her.>

"You belong with us," Rachel said firmly. "You are a human being, Tobias."

<How can you be so sure?> I asked her.

"Because what counts is what is in your head and in your heart," she said with sudden passion. "A person isn't his body. A person isn't what's on the outside."

<Rachel . . . I don't even remember what I looked like.>

I could see that she wanted to cry. But Rachel is a person with strength that runs all the way through her. Maybe that's why I came to see her. I needed someone to be sure. I wanted someone to let me borrow a little of their strength.

She went over to her nightstand and opened the drawer. She rummaged for a minute, then came back to me. She was holding a small photograph. She turned it so I could see.

It was me. The me I used to be.

<I didn't know you had a picture of me,> I said.

She nodded. "It's not a great picture. In real life you look better."

<In real life,> I echoed.

"Tobias, someday the Andalites will return. If they don't, we're all lost, all the human race. If they do come back, I know they'll have some way to return you to your own body."

<I wish I was sure,> I said.

"I am sure," she said. She put every bit of faith into those three words. She wanted me to believe. But I could see the tears that were threatening to well up in her eyes as she lied.

Like I said, hawks don't miss much.

Chapter 13

Talking to Rachel helped. A little, anyway. I spent the night in my little drawer in Jake's attic.

I spent the next day flying around, waiting for my friends to get out of school. In some ways, I realized, my situation wasn't all bad. For one thing, I had no homework. For another, I could fly. How many average kids can get to sixty-five kilometres per hour in level flight and break a hundred and thirty in a stoop — a dive?

I went to the beach and rode the thermals there. It was best where the cliffs pressed right up against the blue ocean.

I saw some prey, some mice and voles in the grass along the top of the cliff, but I ignored them. I was Tobias. I was human.

Jake had called a meeting for all of us for that evening in his room. Tom, Jake's brother, would be away at a meeting of The Sharing.

The Sharing is a "front" for the Yeerks. They pretend it's just some kind of Boy Scouts or whatever, but its real purpose is to recruit voluntary hosts for the Yeerks.

I've got into the habit of checking people's watches from up in the air. Also, you know how banks sometimes will have a big sign showing the time and temperature? Those are helpful, too.

It's strange the things you miss when you lose your human body. Like showers. Like really sleeping, all the way, totally passed out. Or like knowing what time it is.

In the afternoon I flew back to the school. I drifted around overhead till it let out. Then I waited till I saw Jake, Rachel, Cassie, and Marco come out. They came out separately. Marco had pointed out that it was bad security for them to be seen together all the time.

I followed the bus with Jake and Rachel in it. They lived closest, just a few blocks away from each other. Marco lived in some apartments on the other side of the boulevard. He lived with just his dad, since his mum drowned a few years ago.

Cassie had to travel farthest, out to the farm, which was about two kilometres from the others. For me it was about a three-minute flight.

Like I say, there are some good things about having wings. I guess really it's OK most of the time. Really.

I floated on a nice thermal above Jake's house, waiting for him to get home. I saw him get off the bus and go inside. I couldn't see Rachel from where I was because there were trees in the way, but I did see Marco for just a second or two.

I concentrated on watching my friends. That way I didn't notice the squirrels in the trees as much. Or the mice that poked their little noses from their holes and sniffed the air.

After a while I saw Tom leave Jake's house.

Tom looks just like Jake, only he's bigger and has shorter hair. I'd never really known Tom well. But it was during the doomed attempt to rescue him from the Yeerk pool that I was trapped.

He headed down the street, acting nonchalant. Then, a block away, a car pulled up and opened a door. He jumped in.

Off to his meeting of The Sharing.

After a while, I saw the others start to head for Jake's house. I could identify Rachel easily. She was practicing for her gymnastics as she walked. She would walk along the edges of kerbs, pretending they were balance beams.

I flew in Jake's window once everyone was there. I didn't want it to look like I'd been hanging around all that time with nothing to do.

"About time," Marco said. "We've all been waiting here for like an hour."

They'd been there for about two minutes. <I'm a busy bird,> I said. <I lost track of time.>

"We better make this kind of quick," Cassie said. "Ms. Lambert gave us papers to write by day after tomorrow, and I promised my dad I'd help him release this great horned owl. He was a mess. He'd landed on a power line and got fried. But he's ready to go now. We have a habitat picked out."

"Friend of yours, Tobias?" Marco teased me.

The others all shot him nasty looks. But the truth was, it made me feel OK to be teased by Marco. Marco teased everyone.

<We hawks don't hang with owls,> I said. <They do nights, we mostly do days.>

"He's a beautiful animal," Cassie said.

<I see them sometimes at night,> I said. <They're amazing. So cool. Totally silent. Their wings don't make a sound. One can fly just in front of your face and you won't hear it.>

"Um, OK, look, if Cassie has to get going, maybe we better deal with business," Jake said.

"Yeah, if you two are done with the bird-talk part of the meeting," Marco added.

"I have to get going soon, too," Rachel said. She looked a little embarrassed. "My gymnastics class is putting on an exhibition at the mall."

"Oh, I'm *there*," Marco crowed.

"No, you are *not* there," Rachel snapped. "None of you is going near that place. You know how I feel about having to put on stupid exhibitions."

Rachel is not one of those people who like to perform in front of a crowd.

"We have learned how the Yeerks get their air and water," Jake said, trying to get down to business. "And we even know where they do it. And we more or less know when. There ought to be some way for us to use this information. Any ideas?"

Rachel shrugged. "We try and find a way to destroy the ship."

Marco raised his hand like he was in class. "How about if we, um, go back to talking about birds?"

Rachel ignored him, as she usually did. "Look, we find some way to destroy that ship and maybe the Yeerks will run out of air and water. Maybe that will even mean that they have to give up and go home."

"Maybe," Cassie said. "Or they may have a dozen more of those ships in different places all over the earth. We don't know how many ships they have."

"This one would be all we need if — " Marco began to say. Then I guess he realized he was about to suggest something dangerous. "I mean . . . nothing."

"What?" Jake asked him. "What were you going to say?"

Marco looked trapped. He shrugged. "Okay, look, what if that ship didn't get blown up or disintegrated or whatever. What if it was flying over the city and suddenly the cloaking device was turned off?"

We were all silent while we thought about that image. Suddenly a million people would look up in the sky and see a ship the size of a skyscraper.

"People would probably notice it," Jake said.

"Oh yeah, they would notice it," Rachel agreed. "Radar would see it, too. A million eyewitnesses. The Controllers would never be able to cover it up!"

<People would videotape it,> I said. <They would take pictures. There would be radar tapes.>

Jake grinned. "The whole world would see. The entire human race would realize what was happening." He was getting excited now. "And *then* we could go to the authorities. The Controllers wouldn't be able to stop us! We could tell all we know!"

Rachel's eyes were gleaming. "We could tell them about The Sharing. We could turn in Chapman!"

"And you figure Visser Three and his pals are

just going to sit around and do nothing?" Marco asked. "Like you said, we have no idea how many ships they have. Or how much power."

Jake looked a little disappointed.

<They don't have enough power to attack Earth openly,> I said.

"And how do you know that?" Marco asked.

<Because they are going to a lot of trouble to keep themselves a big secret. You don't hide if you're tough enough to come out and kick butt in a fair fight.>

I expected Marco to have some smart comeback. But he just nodded. "Yeah, you're right."

"This could be our big chance," Rachel said. "Uncloak that ship, so the whole world can see."

"I hate to ask this," Marco said with a groan, "but how do you think you're going to do that?"

It was Jake who answered. "We'll have to get inside that ship." He winked at Marco. "Want to know how?"

Marco shook his head. "Not really."

"Through the water pipes. As fish."

Marco sighed. "Jake, I just *told* you I didn't want to know."

Chapter 14

Rachel and Cassie took off, heading in different directions.

"Have a good show," Cassie called to Rachel.

"Yeah, right," Rachel said grumpily.

"I'll be there soon," Marco told Rachel. "Don't fall off any balance beams until I get there."

Rachel shot Marco one of her "you're a dead man if you mess with me" looks and disappeared, leaving just Marco, Jake, and me.

"She really kind of likes me," Marco said, with a wink at Jake and me.

"Uh-uh," Jake said dryly. "Look, Tobias, if we're going to do this mission, it can't be till the weekend."

<Why?>

"The timing. We have to morph to travel up there. There are no buses and we can't walk that far in human bodies. Even as wolves, though, it takes time. It took more than an hour last time. It just seemed to me that we might want to get up there in the morning, camp out somewhere hidden, and then be ready by afternoon when the Yeerks show up."

"And this time we may want to travel *around* that other wolf pack's territory," Marco pointed out. "I don't want to get into it with them again."

It made sense. <I guess you're right. So if you're going to camp early in the day, you need a Saturday.>

"Anyway, it might be a good idea if we had as much information about the area as we can get." Jake gave me a thoughtful look. "So I was thinking — "

<Yeah,> I interrupted. <I'll spy out the situation. I'll look for someplace you can hide. I have a lot of time on my hands. No hands, exactly, but lots of time.>

Marco and Jake both laughed. I think Marco was surprised that I could make a joke about myself.

I saw an intense look in Jake's eyes. He was wondering if I was OK.

<I'm cool,> I thought-spoke privately to him, so Marco couldn't hear. <I was just a little

weirded-out by watching you all struggle to get out of those wolf morphs.>

He raised an eyebrow and nodded. He had been upset, too. I could imagine. I suspected there had been a lot of nightmares over that mess.

"Okay, so now what?" Marco asked. "Do I sneak into the mall without Rachel being able to see me, or do we all sit around and play Doom?"

"I have homework," Jake said. "And trust me, Marco, if Rachel sees you at the mall making faces while she's on the balance beam, she will turn into an elephant and stomp you."

Marco winced. "Remember the good old days when all a girl could do to you was call you names?"

I flew off, leaving them to play video games or do homework, or however they ended up killing time. Either way, it wasn't something I could participate in.

It's kind of a shame, really. With my eyesight and the reaction time I have, I could probably be major competition in Doom.

But joysticks and control pads aren't made for talons.

I swooped out into the cool afternoon.

I drifted around for a while. I checked out Chapman's house. Mr Chapman is our assistant principal. He's also one of the highest-ranking Controllers.

When we first learned Chapman was one of *them*, he was ordering a Hork-Bajir to kill any of us who were caught. He told the Hork-Bajir to save our heads for identification. Not the kind of thing you expect to hear.

Even from an assistant principal.

But it turned out things were more complicated than we thought. Chapman had joined the Yeerks. But he had done it in part to save his daughter, Melissa.

Melissa would be at the gymnastics thing with Rachel. At the mall.

Remembering the mall made me sad. It was just another one of the places I couldn't go any more. There was a long list: school, cinemas, amusement parks . . .

Wait a minute. I *could* go to the amusement park. And I wouldn't even have to pay admission.

The thought made me happy. I don't know why. It wasn't like I could ride the roller coaster. But still, the idea kind of perked me up.

I could bust right into The Gardens any time I wanted. Come to think of it, I could also watch any football or baseball game I ever wanted to see, too, as long as it was outdoors.

And concerts!

Whoa! Big stadium concerts, no problem. No tickets needed.

That's the way I needed to be thinking. There were millions of things I could do as a bird that I couldn't do as a human.

But not right now. I turned and headed towards the mountains. I had a job to do. It was another good thing about being me. I was the ultimate airborne spy.

There was a long line of towering clouds running to the mountains. Perfect weather for me. Thermals are what push those clouds up so high.

I just let myself get into it. It wasn't a bad life. Not really.

I was flying. Back when I was in my old body, I used to look up in the sky and wish I could fly. Now I could. I figured there were probably kids down on the ground right now looking up at me and thinking, "Wow, that would be so cool."

If only I had something to eat. I was feeling a little hungry. Should have asked Jake to grab me a snack.

It happened before I really even had time to think about it. I guess it was because I was feeling good. Feeling relaxed.

I was above the woods, just a kilometre or so beyond Cassie's farm. The trees opened up to form a little meadow. This is what red-tails love. A little meadow.

It was full of prey. Squirrels scouring the ground for nuts. Hopping, then sitting up on their hind legs to look around nervously. Mice that scurried from hole to hole. Rabbits.

A rat.

My eyes focused on it with absolute intensity. I sort of shrugged one shoulder, turned sharply in midair, and plummeted towards the earth in a stoop.

My wings were back. My head low. My talons tucked back for maximum speed.

Sudden flare! I opened my wings. The shock of the air. Talons raked forward. Eyes never moving even a millimetre from the rat.

Focus!

I struck!

An incredible rush of excitement surged through me. I was ecstatic! Ecstatic! That's the only word for it. It was intense beyond anything I had ever experienced.

Talons hit warm flesh. My razor claws squeezed. The rat squirmed in my grip. But it was helpless! Helpless!

I was in a frenzy.

I hooded my wings around my kill, shielding it from any other predator that might try to steal it away.

<NO! NO! NO! NO! **NO!**>

I fell back.

I looked down at my talons. They were red with blood.

Rat meat dripped from my beak.

In my panic, I forgot what I was. I tried to run away. But I no longer had legs and feet to run with. I had killing talons. Bloody talons.

I fell in the dirt.

No, I cried voicelessly. But I could still see the dead rat. And I could taste it. And no matter how many times I said "no," it would always be "yes."

Chapter 15

I flew.

I flew as fast and as hard as I could. I wanted to go so fast that the memory of killing and eating the rat would be left way behind me.

But not even I can fly that fast.

Human! I am human! I am Tobias!

I don't know why it was Rachel I wanted to see right at that moment. Maybe she was just the closest thing I had to a real friend. Maybe it was the way she had seemed so sure of who and what I was.

I needed someone to be sure.

Down below I saw the huge, irregular rectangles of the shopping mall. I saw a glass door.

People streamed in and out. Rachel. That's where she was.

"Tseeeeer!"

I screamed in rage and frustration and terror as I stooped. I shot towards the door like I'd shot towards the rat.

But I wasn't going to stop. I wasn't going to slow down. I was just going to end this right now. I would hit the glass at full speed and maybe that would awaken me from this nightmare.

The speed just kept building. The door rushed up at me. The earth itself was jumping up to hit me.

A guy, dark hair, short, stepped to the door. He opened it.

Shwoooop!

I must have been doing eighty as I hurtled through the open door.

A second set of doors, but these were open, too.

No impact.

No awakening.

Colours and bright lights all around me. Like a high-speed kaleidoscope.

The Gap. Express. The Body Shop. Easy Spirit. Mrs. Fields.

Zoom!

I was a bullet, blazing centimetres over the

heads of the shoppers. I heard screams. I heard cries of amazement.

I didn't care. I wanted to hit something. I wanted to wake up. I wanted to fall to the ground because my wings had disappeared and been replaced by clumsy legs and flailing arms.

I wanted to be me again.

I am human! I am human! I am Tobias!

Nine West. Radio Shack. B. Dalton. Benetton. A world I knew. A world where I belonged. Places I had been. Foods I had eaten. The world of human beings.

Zoom!

Suddenly, in seconds, I was at the centre of the mall.

A crowd was standing around in a circle. In the middle of the circle blue mats were on the floor. Girls in leotards were doing midair flips and graceful backbends. People on the upper level were crowded around the railing to look down.

Rachel was on the balance beam. She was just raising one leg, balancing on the other.

I was a brown and gold and red missile shooting past her.

"Tobias!" she cried.

Straight ahead, a wall. A blank wall where they were going to put a new shop. I was still

89

moving fast. I could still hit it and wake myself up from the nightmare.

"No!" Rachel cried.

I flared and shot straight up. The wall scraped my stomach. The ceiling was glass, a skylight. I was there! A last-second turn, almost too late. My shoulder hit the glass. I bounced off and began to fall down towards upraised faces staring at me with horror and amazement and pity.

I saw Rachel's face in that crowd. Her eyes pleaded silently. No, she mouthed. No.

I fell, stunned and dazed. Rachel, still balanced on the beam, caught me as I dropped. She fell off and the two of us tumbled on to the mat.

"You have to get out of here!" she muttered tersely.

<I killed,> I cried. <You don't understand, Rachel. I'm lost. I *killed*!>

"No. As long as you have me and the others, you aren't lost, Tobias."

Helping hands were clawing, trying to save Rachel from the crazed, out-of-control bird. She gave me a heave. Just enough to get me into the air. Anyone watching would have thought she was trying to get me off her.

I flapped up, just out of reach of a dozen hands that clawed the air trying to grab me. Someone threw a shopping bag at me. I dodged.

But there was no escape. Overhead I saw the

90

skylight. Blue sky.

The hawk in my head wanted the sky. It knew safety was up in the high blue. The hawk powered straight up. Straight up at the glass that he didn't understand. The glass that would be like a brick wall.

But I couldn't fight it any more. The hawk had won. I had killed. I had killed and eaten. And I had loved it. The ecstasy of the hunt.

Ecstasy!

In a second it would all be over. One more stroke of my powerful wings and the glass . . .

Out of the corner of my eye I saw a familiar face on the upper level. Suddenly, something shot past me. Small, white, stitched.

CRASH!

The baseball hit the glass just centimetres ahead of my beak. Just where Marco had aimed it. Glass shards fell around me. I shot through the hole.

Sky!

The hawk flew fast and straight.

I let it go. I surrendered.

Tobias, a boy whose face I could no longer remember, no longer existed.

Chapter 16

The next few days were like a long, slow dream. I stayed away from Jake's house. I did not communicate with my friends. I disappeared.

I found a place for myself. It was perfect redtail territory — the place where I had made my first kill. A nice meadow surrounded by trees. Not far off there was a marshy area that was good, too. Although there was another red-tail who had a territory over there, so I couldn't hunt there often.

I spent my days hunting. Sometimes I would ride the high hot winds and watch the meadow. Sometimes I would sit in a tree and watch till some unwary creature ventured out. Then I would swoop down on it, snatch it up, kill it. Eat it while the blood was still warm.

Days were easier than nights. During the day I was hunting almost all the time. It keeps you busy, because most of the time you miss. It can take quite a few tries before you make a kill.

Nights were worse. I couldn't hunt at night. The nights belong to other predators, mostly the owls. At night my human mind would surface.

The human in my head would show me memories. Pictures of human life. Pictures of his friends. The human in my head was sad. Lonely.

But the human Tobias really just wanted to sleep. He wanted to disappear and let the hawk rule. He wanted to accept that he was no longer human.

Still, at night, as I sat on my familiar branch and watched the owls do their silent, deadly work, the human memories would play in my head.

But other memories were there, too. I remembered the female hawk. The one who had been in the cage. I knew where her territory was. Near a clear lake in the mountains.

So one day I flew there. To the mountain lake.

I saw her down on a tree branch. She was watching a baby raccoon, preparing to go for a kill. She would have to be very hungry to go for a raccoon, no matter how small. Raccoons are very tough, very violent creatures.

As I watched, unnoticed by her, she swooped.

93

The raccoon spotted her. A quick dodge left, and the hawk sailed harmlessly past. The baby raccoon ran for the edge of the woods. His mother was there.

No hawk was crazy enough to go after a full-grown raccoon. That was not a fight the hawk was going to win.

She settled back on her branch.

I floated overhead, waiting to see if she would spot me. And waiting to see what she would do when she did notice me. I had to be cautious. She was a female, and females are a third bigger, on average, than males.

Suddenly I saw fast movement in the woods. A chase!

It was always kind of exciting watching a kill, even by another species. It heightened my own hunting edge.

The prey was running awkwardly on its two legs. Running and threading its way through the underbrush. It stumbled and hit the ground hard. It seemed very slow to get up. It ran again.

I could hear gasping breath. It was weakening. The prey was squealing. Loud, yelping vocalizations.

Prey often squeal.

The predator moved on two legs also. But these legs were built for greater speed. It had blades growing from its arms. It used the blades to slash the bushes and weeds. It cleared its way through them like a lawn mower chopping down tall grass.

Lawn mower?

No. Something else. Salad Shooter. Yes, that's what Marco called them.

Marco? The image came to my mind. Short. Dark hair. Human.

It hit me like a lightning bolt. Suddenly I realized: This prey was a *human*.

Why should I care? It was prey. That was the way it worked: Predator killed prey.

NO! It was a human being.

"Help! Help!" That was the vocalization. It meant something. "Help! Help me!"

The predator was very close. In a few seconds he would make his kill. The predator was powerful. The predator was swift.

Hork-Bajir.

"Help me, someone help!"

I don't know how to describe what happened next. It was like my entire world flipped over. Like one minute it was one thing, one way, then, boom, it was something totally different. It was like opening your eyes after a dream.

The prey was a human being. The predator was a Hork-Bajir. This was wrong. Wrong! It had to be stopped.

I stopped.

A few seconds earlier I was thinking that no sane hawk would go after a full-grown raccoon. Now I was going after a Hork-Bajir. Hork-Bajir compare to raccoons like a nuclear bomb compares to a bow and arrow.

It would have to be the eyes. The eyes were the only weak spot.

"Tseeeeer!"

I rocketed towards the Hork-Bajir. The human slipped and fell again.

Talons forward. The Hork-Bajir was totally focused on his prey. I hit him fast and hard and sailed past.

"Gurrawwwrr!" the Hork-Bajir yelled. He clutched at his eyes.

The human was up and running again.

"Gurr gafrasch! To me! Getting away! Hilch nahurrn!" the Hork-Bajir yelled, in the strange combination of human and alien speech that they use when working with humans.

He was calling for help. I used my momentum to soar up over the tops of the trees. He had plenty of help available. Another Hork-Bajir about a thousand metres off. And two of the bogus Park Rangers were nearer.

It was all coming back to me. The fake Park Rangers. The Hork-Bajir enforcers. This was the lake. A Yeerk supply ship must be on its way in.

Yeerks. Andalites.

My friends, the Animorphs.

Yes, my *friends*. I remembered now. But this human was not one of them. This human prey was older. A stranger.

The freed hawk was watching me. I could almost feel her drawing me towards her. It was like a magnet. She was my kind. She was like me.

But the Park Rangers were in hot pursuit of the human now. The human was nothing like me. Poor, clumsy ground runner that he was. He was just prey.

And yet, for some reason, I couldn't let him be prey.

I couldn't. *Me.*

Tobias.

Chapter 17

I landed on the perch outside Rachel's window. It was night. But she wasn't asleep. She was reading a book in bed, sitting propped up by a few pillows.

I fluttered a wing against the glass.

<Rachel?>

She started. The book went flying. She jumped up and ran to the window, throwing it open.

"Tobias?"

<More or less,> I said wryly.

She started to hug me, to put her arms around me. But then she realized that wasn't possible. Birds aren't exactly made for hugging.

"Are you OK? We've all been terrified. Cassie said maybe you were killed or something. There are all kinds of things that can happen. Jake is so depressed."

<I'm OK,> I said. I flapped over to her dresser.

Now that she was sure I was safe, she started getting mad. It made me smile inwardly. That was Rachel for you.

"Tobias, what is the deal with you? Why would you just disappear and leave us all worrying for days?"

<It's hard to explain,> I said. <I guess . . . the hawk sort of won out over me. Not that it's really that way. I mean, the hawk instincts . . . they're strong.> I told her about my first kill. About how much it horrified me.

I don't know how I expected her to react. She tried to look sympathetic, but I could see it bothered her.

<I lost control,> I admitted. <For the last couple of days I've been living like a hawk. All the way, like a hawk. I was starting to forget . . . me. I was starting to lose touch with humans. Then something happened.>

"What?" She went to check her door and make sure neither of her sisters was nearby. I could hear that the house was quiet. "What happened?"

I told her about going to the lake. I told her about the guy being chased by Hork-Bajir.

<Fortunately, I can see the terrain better than the Hork-Bajir or those human-Controller Park Rangers. I led him away from them. I told him when to hide and when to run.>

"You talked to him?"

<I thought-spoke, yes. There was no alternative. I couldn't let them catch him. He had seen a Hork-Bajir. They would never have let him live.>

Rachel looked stunned. "But now he knows about you! And he knows about the Hork-Bajir."

<What's he going to do? Go tell people he was chased through the woods by an alien monster, and rescued by a telepathic bird?>

Rachel laughed. "Yeah, good point. People would just think he was insane. Besides, if he started talking openly about the Yeerks, they would find him and silence him."

<Exactly what I explained to him. I think he'll probably keep quiet. He'll try to forget it ever happened.>

"You saved him," Rachel said.

<I almost didn't,> I admitted. <At first I just saw another predator and his prey. No different from watching the owls at night. No different from what I do myself. Kill to eat.>

Rachel thought about that for a moment. "The Yeerks and their slaves aren't killing to eat," she said. "They are killing to control and dominate. Killing because it's the only way you can eat, because that's the way nature designed you, that's one thing. Killing because you want power or control is evil."

<I guess you're right,> I said. <I hadn't thought about it that way.>

"What you did . . . eating . . . you know, whatever. Well, that's natural for the hawk. Nothing a Hork-Bajir does is natural. They aren't even in control of their own bodies or minds. They are tools of the Yeerks. And the Yeerks only want power and domination."

<I know,> I said. But I wasn't totally convinced. Still, it was comforting to be talking to Rachel.

"You are *human*, Tobias," she told me softly.

<Yeah. Maybe. I don't know. Sometimes I just feel so trapped. I want to move my fingers, but I don't have any. I want to speak out loud, but I have a mouth that's only good for ripping and tearing.>

Rachel looked like she might start crying. It was alarming to me, because Rachel isn't a girl who bursts out in tears, ever.

<Anyway, look, I'm sorry I ruined your exhibition at the mall the other day.>

She smiled. "What do you mean? Your timing

was perfect. I was just starting my routine, and you know how much I hate public shows like that. You put an end to the whole thing real fast."

I laughed silently. <I can imagine. I hope no one was hurt by the falling glass.>

"No, everyone was fine. But what were you going to do if Marco had missed with that baseball? You would have hit the glass awfully hard."

I didn't know what to say.

Rachel came closer and stroked my crest with her hand. It made the hawk in me uncomfortable. But at the same time, it was similar to preening, which is kind of pleasurable.

"What I told you the other day, Tobias . . . remember? You're not lost as long as you have Jake and Cassie and me. Even Marco. He came through for you, big time. We're your friends. You're not alone."

I think I would have cried then. But hawks can't cry.

"And someday, the Andalites will come. . . ."

<Someday,> I said, trying to sound confident. <Well, I better go see Jake. The mission is supposed to begin tomorrow.>

"We don't have to go through with that," Rachel said.

<Yes, we do,> I said. <More than ever, I understand that. See . . . there are human beings all over, trapped in bodies controlled by Yeerks.

Trapped. Unable to escape. Rachel, I know how they feel. Maybe I can't escape. Maybe I am trapped forever. But if we can free some of those others. Maybe . . . I don't know. Maybe that's what I need to do to stay human.>

Chapter 18

The next day, we went ahead with the mission. I flew cover overhead while four grey wolves ran beneath me. We timed it so we would arrive in the area very early in the morning, many hours before the Yeerks would arrive to hunt intruders.

<So, let me get this straight, Tobias,> Marco said. <You're taking us to a bear cave? As in big grizzly bears? And this is a good thing?>

<Not grizzlies,> Cassie interrupted. <Not in this area. We'd be talking black bears. They're much smaller.>

<Swell. I am totally reassured. Just a *small* bear cave.>

<The bears are long gone,> I said. <There are

just a few bears around, and this cave is empty. Trust me. I spied it out yesterday. I've seen raccoons and skunks running in and out of there. They wouldn't be doing that if there were bears.>

<Excuse me. Jake? Did Tobias just say 'skunks'? I must have heard wrong, because only an idiot would think hanging out with skunks is a good idea.>

<We're not going to hang out with skunks,> Jake said patiently.

<The skunks don't live there,> I said. <They just run in there to get away from predators.>

I didn't have to explain any more. I think everyone guessed how I knew that skunks ran in there to get away from predators.

<Look, it's close to the lake but I don't think the Yeerks know about it,> I said. <Sorry, but there wasn't a convenient Marriott hotel where I could get you a room for the night.>

<So, that means no room service, either?> Marco asked. <Well, OK. As long as this cave gets cable. The big game's on tonight.>

I was carrying a tiny nylon pouch that Rachel had put together. It was tan in colour, so a casual observer wouldn't notice it and wonder why a red-tail hawk was carrying luggage.

In the sack was a small watch. It weighed almost nothing. There were also some fish hooks, fishing line, and a small lighter. All together it only weighed a few grammes. But it did slow me down a little.

We reached the cave with plenty of time to spare on the two-hour deadline.

<Oh, this looks lovely,> Marco said, looking at the thorns and a scrub brush around the cave entrance.

<I haven't really been inside,> I admitted.

I landed outside the entrance. The opening to the cave was no more than a metre across and about a metre and a half high. It was easy for Jake and Rachel, in their wolf morphs, to leap nimbly through. Unless there really was a bear inside, they would scare off anything in there.

<Empty,> Rachel reported. <Nothing in here but a couple of spiders and a scared mouse.>

I decided to try a joke. <Chase him out here. I'm hungry.>

Only Marco laughed. The others all acted like I'd said something embarrassing. Maybe I had.

<Let's morph back,> Marco suggested. <One close call with being trapped as a wolf is plenty for me.>

<I'll go look around,> I said. Sometimes I didn't like being there when they morphed.

A few minutes later they all came out. Marco was complaining, as usual. "You know, we really have to figure out how to deal with the footwear

106

situation," he muttered. "Thorns and no shoes. Not a good combination."

The four of them were barefoot and dressed only in their morphing outfits: leotards for the girls, bike shorts and tight T-shirts for Jake and Marco.

"We need to gather firewood," Jake said, with his hands on his hips. "It wouldn't hurt to warm that cave up a little before the Yeerks get here."

"Don't you love it when Jake's all masterful like that?" Rachel teased.

"I'm just trying to get us organized," Jake said defensively.

"We'd better get started fishing," Cassie pointed out. "If we don't catch a fish, we're pretty much wasting our time."

The plan was to morph into fish to enter the Yeerk ship's water pipes. Of course, in order to morph into something, you first have to "acquire" it. Which means being able to touch it.

"Shouldn't be any big problem," Jake said confidently.

"Uh-huh," Cassie said dryly. "And how many times have you gone fishing?"

"Counting this time? Once." He laughed.

Cassie rolled her eyes. "Typical suburban boy," she said affectionately. "It isn't all that easy."

<Then you guys better get started,> I advised. <I'll go look around.>

"Take care of yourself, Tobias," Rachel called out as I took wing.

I watched from on high as they made one failed attempt after another to convince a fish to bite one of our hooks.

It seemed ridiculous, but the entire plan was hanging on the question of whether or not we could catch a fish. And time was running out. The day wore on. Still no fish.

Jake was getting edgy. Rachel was downright cranky. And Marco? Forget Marco. "This is ridiculous!" he raged. "We're four — I mean, five — fairly intelligent human beings. And we can't outsmart one fish that probably has an IQ of four?"

Cassie was the only one remaining calm. "Fishing is a matter of skill and luck," she said placidly. "A smart fisherman learns not to become frustrated."

Jake looked at the little watch we'd brought along. "From what we know, the Yeerks will start arriving in an hour to clear the area."

Rachel nodded. "Even if we catch a fish now, we won't have time to test the morph."

<Maybe we should back off for today,> I suggested. <You really ought to test out the fish morph. You guys all know how much trouble a morph can be at first.>

Jake shook his head firmly. "I don't think so,

Tobias. We'd have to wait till we had another day off. Tomorrow's no good because I have stuff with my parents. So does Marco. Which means we'd have to wait a whole week."

<So we try again next weekend. What's the hurry?>

"The hurry is that the Yeerks can't keep coming to this same lake forever. Sooner or later the level of the water will start dropping, from them taking so much. They must use one lake for a while, then move on to another. It could take forever for us to find where they move to next."

It made sense. But that didn't make me feel any better about it.

<This is the first water animal any of us have morphed. You don't have any idea what it's going to be like.>

"I know," Jake snapped. "Look, Tobias, I know it's not exactly ideal."

"Hah!" Cassie yelped. She yanked at the line she was holding. "I believe we may have a fishy."

It took just a few seconds to haul in the fish.

"Trout," she said as it flopped in the shallow water. The hook was poked through its lip. It was about twenty-five centimetres long, not very big.

The four of them stared blankly at it.

"We have to become *that*?" Marco asked.

"It's a fish," Cassie said. "What else did you expect?"

Marco shrugged. "I don't know. Something more like *Jaws*. This is just a fish. I mean, we could clean him and eat him with a little lemon juice. Maybe some fries on the side."

The others turned and gave him a dirty look.

Cassie reached down into the water and took hold of the squirmy grey thing. She concentrated. Her eyes closed halfway. She was acquiring it. The fish DNA was being absorbed into Cassie's body.

The gift of the Andalite. The curse of the Andalite — the power to morph.

Chapter 19

<I don't like this plan,> I blurted.

Jake looked up at me in surprise. "Tobias, you were in on the planning right from the start."

<Look, don't you guys realize how dangerous this could be?>

"I realize," Marco said. "I realize it plenty. But I thought you were the big, gung-ho Yeerk-killer. Suddenly now you're afraid?"

<I'm not afraid for me,> I said. <I'll be flying around safely while the four of you go up into that ship.>

Cassie nodded. "It's hard standing by while someone else is risking their life," she said. "I understand how you feel. But there have been times when *you* were the one taking the risks."

111

"Look, we don't have time to debate this," Jake said. "We have a plan we've all agreed to. Let's get on with it before the Yeerks show up." Jake gets peevish when someone questions things after everything has already been decided. Usually it's Marco getting on his nerves.

"We'll be OK," Rachel said confidently. Rachel took the fish in her hand. The fish went limp, as usual, while the acquiring was happening.

Suddenly I couldn't watch any more. I'd just had a flash of memory, watching the four of them straining to get out of their wolf bodies. What if they were trapped in fish morph?

The idea of being trapped was still not something any of them really understood. I mean, they knew it had happened to me. But people are funny — they never think something bad will happen to *them.* I knew it could happen.

And to be trapped as a fish? It made me sick just thinking about it. The rest of your life in the body of a fish? Being trapped in a hawk's body seemed downright pleasant by comparison.

<I'm going to go upstairs and see if anyone's coming,> I said. I caught a small breeze and flapped hard to clear the treetops.

It was tough work gaining enough altitude to get a good view of the area. It was mostly dead air all around. But I was glad for the workout. It took my mind off imagining what life would be like if my only friends in the world were trapped as fish in a mountain lake.

I would have laughed if it weren't so serious. I mean, come on, how many kids have to worry about all their friends becoming fish? Life had definitely got strange since that night when we saw the Andalite landing in the construction site.

I circled higher and higher till I could see the entire lake and most of the surrounding area. No Park Rangers. Yet. I wondered if Jake was right and maybe the Yeerks would move on to another lake. Maybe they already had.

Then, there, way down below, on a branch . . . the hawk. The female I had freed from captivity.

She was watching me. I could see her eyes follow me across the sky. In part, I knew, she was merely watching me for the simple reason that I was in her territory. Hawks are defensive about their territory. They don't want strangers coming and grabbing all the best prey.

But I had the feeling that there was something more going on. She wanted me to join her. I don't know how I knew that, but I did. She wanted me to fly down to her.

Some people think hawks mate for just the

one season. Some people think they mate for life, and I don't really know which is true.

One thing I knew for sure: I wasn't ready to settle down with anyone. Especially not a hawk.

And yet there was this feeling in me. Like . . . like I *belonged* with her.

I looked away. I would be glad when this mission was over and I no longer had to come here to her territory. She confused me.

Suddenly, movement!

I had let myself be distracted.

Trucks! Jeeps! They were rolling down the road. They were within a kilometre and moving fast.

I looked frantically for my friends. There they were! I shrugged off the wind beneath my wings and dropped towards them.

<Here they come!> I cried. <Get to the cave!>

They ran for the cave. But it was harder to crawl inside in their human bodies. The wolves' thick pelts had protected them against the scratches and tears of the bushes.

Thwak thwak thwak thwak thwak!

Helicopters skimming above the trees!

Too fast. My friends were still struggling to make it to the shelter of the cave. One of the helicopters was on a straight line to them.

<Oh, man,> I muttered. I still had a lot of my

114

speed from the dive. I flapped hard, powering up to maximum speed. Straight at the helicopter.

Straight at it.

I could see the pilot. A human-Controller. Beside him sat a Hork-Bajir.

Straight at them!

The chopper was doing ninety. I was doing a little less. The distance between me and the chopper's windshield shortened very fast.

They weren't going to pull up!

Chapter 20

*T*hwak thwak thwak thwak thwak!

The sound of the rotors was a roar.

They were not going to pull up! We were going to hit.

But then, a flicker of the pilot's eyes, a twitch of his hand on the control stick.

I cranked right.

The helicopter cranked left.

It blew past me like a tornado. The backwash of the rotors caught me and tumbled me through the air.

I fell, upside down. I folded my wings, flared my tail, and spun around. I opened my wings and swooped neatly between two trees.

I banked left and flew over the cave. Rachel was the last one in. She was still clearly visible. The helicopter would almost certainly have seen her.

I watched till she was safely inside.

<Okay, you guys, I don't think anyone saw you. Be cool till I tell you it's time.>

They couldn't answer, of course. They were still fully human, so they could hear my thought-speech, but could not respond in kind.

The Yeerks went through the familiar routine. The fake Park Rangers fanned out around the lake with automatic weapons ready. The helicopters buzzed around until they decided the area was free of witnesses.

The helicopters landed and the Hork-Bajir jumped out. They seemed extra careful. Probably Visser Three had given them all kinds of grief over the guy I had helped to escape the day before.

Visser Three was not a creature you wanted mad at you.

Then, I felt it. The emptiness in the sky. The sense of something monstrously huge moving slowly through the air.

It was above me.

Slowly it appeared, shimmering into reality like some kind of magic trick.

117

You could never get used to how big that thing was. It felt like someone was hanging a small moon over your head.

I flew out from under it, over closer to the cave. <It's here,> I announced.

From behind the truck ship came the usual guard of Bug fighters. Only instead of two Bug fighters, there were four. The Yeerks were definitely nervous this time. Two of the Bug fighters remained on patrol. The other two landed in the clearing beside the helicopters.

Why? Why the extra security? Was it just because of the guy I had helped to escape?

I felt something new in the air above the hovering truck ship. Another cloaked ship!

Not as large, but from that emptiness in the sky I felt a dread that I had felt before.

The cloak shimmered out and the ship appeared.

Black within black, an outthrust spear, razor-edged — I had seen this ship before. The Blade ship! I had seen it first at the construction site where the Andalite had been murdered while we cried helplessly.

No wonder the Yeerks were nervous.

The Blade ship lowered towards the landing area. The Hork-Bajir on the ground and the Park Rangers were in a frenzy now, searching the woods as if their lives depended on it.

118

Tssewww!

Someone had fired a Dracon beam. I looked and saw a deer in mid-leap sizzle and disappear. The Yeerks were shooting anything that moved.

The doors of the Blade ship opened. More Hork-Bajir poured out, Dracon beams levelled. Behind them came a pair of Taxxons, slithering and shimmying on their needle legs, undulating their gross caterpillar bodies.

And last, he stepped out: dainty Andalite hooves. Deadly Andalite tail, like a scorpion's. The mouthless Andalite face. The two small Andalite arms with too many fingers. The two mobile eyes mounted on antlerlike stalks that turned this way and that, always searching, so that the large main eyes could focus on one thing at a time.

An Andalite body.

But not an Andalite mind. For in that Andalite body lived a Yeerk. The only Andalite-Controller. The only Yeerk ever to enslave an Andalite. And thus, the only Yeerk to have the power to morph.

I dropped down into the trees. I waited till a patrolling Hork-Bajir had walked past the cave where my friends hid.

When I was sure no one would see, I fluttered down and into the cave, scraping the bushes on either side.

"Tobias? Is that you?" Jake whispered.

<Yes.>

"What are you doing here? That's not the plan."

<Forget the plan. *He's* here.>

No one asked who. They all knew from the way I had said it.

He was here.

Visser Three.

120

Chapter 21

<What is *he* doing here?" Cassie asked in a low, frightened whisper.

<I guess he just came to oversee this trip. Maybe it was because they let that guy get away.>

"He's here to kick his boys," Marco said, trying to sound tough. "They screwed up badly, and now he's here to make sure they don't do it again."

<It doesn't really matter *why* he's here,> I pointed out. <He's here. And there are extra Hork-Bajir and the whole crowd is way nervous. One of the Hork-Bajir Draconed a deer that just happened to be walking by.>

"A deer?" Cassie cried. "Those stupid jerks.

121

Deer never hurt anyone."

<The plan was for you to sneak down to the water, morph as soon as you got there, and head out for the ship's water-intake pipe,> I reminded them. <It was always a dangerous plan, but now it's impossible. Four of you walking down to the water, then morphing? That's not going to happen. Not as alert as these guys are now.>

"Not with Visser Three hanging around," Marco agreed.

"I disagree." It was Rachel. "I think we should still try this. Look, if we pull this off, if we manage to get inside that ship and disable the cloaking device while they're over the city . . . this whole thing will be over."

Jake jumped in to support her. "We've always said, if there was just some way to show the world what was happening . . . well, this is the way. This would be way too big for the Controllers to cover up. I don't care *who* they are. Even if the mayor and the governor and the entire police force were Controllers, they couldn't cover up something like this."

<Jake, you're not listening. I'm telling you: there is no way you four can cruise down to the lake. You'll be dead before you take five steps!>

For a while no one spoke. It was Cassie who finally broke the silence. "There may be a way," she said. "See, a fish can survive out of water for a couple of minutes. And the fish we're morphing is small." She looked at me. "Small enough for a red-tailed hawk to carry."

Well. That idea got everyone's attention, I can tell you.

"Excuse me?" Marco shrilled. "Are you saying you want me to not just morph into a fish, but to morph into a fish *out of water* and then be carried through the air by a bird?"

Cassie bit her lip. "I'm just saying it could work."

"It would work," Jake said. He and Rachel exchanged a slightly insane look that said, "Okay, let's try it!"

<No way,> I said. <You guys are totally crazy. No offence, but this raises the danger level way beyond what it was to start with.>

"I know it's dangerous," Jake said. "But we may never get a chance this good."

Marco whined. I argued. But in the end it was three against two. Besides, Jake was right: we had a chance to seriously mess up the Yeerks.

I have watched Marco morph into a gorilla, Rachel become an elephant and a shrew and a cat, Cassie become a horse, and Jake become a tiger and a flea (man, was *that* weird!). But this was the first time anyone had tried morphing into an animal that lived in water.

Cassie insisted on going first. "It was my

123

idea," she pointed out. She did not point out that she was also the best morpher.

"If you feel like you're suffocating, you have to back out of the morph," Jake told her. He took her hand. "Are you listening to me? You have to back out if it gets bad. You can't pass out halfway into a morph."

Cassie smiled. "I will. Don't worry about me."

She closed her eyes and began to concentrate.

I've told you that Cassie is always the best at controlling a morph. She has an almost artistic talent, where she can make it all look kind of cool and not so gross.

But not this time.

As I watched, her hair disappeared completely. Her skin began to harden, like it was coated with varnish or something. Like she had been dipped in clear plastic.

Her eyes swung around to the side of her head. Her face bulged out into a huge mouth that gaped and seemed to be blowing invisible bubbles.

As this happened, she was shrinking. But not fast enough. I could still see every nightmare change in her body. The way her legs shrivelled up, smaller and smaller, till her legless body fell to the ground.

From her lower back her body stretched out,

elongated.

"Ooohhh!" Rachel cried.

A tail had just suddenly spurted from Cassie's behind. A fish tail.

Now her varnished-looking skin cracked and split into a million scales.

Her ears had gone. Her arms were shrivelling. She was no more than half a metre long, lying helpless, a monster, on the floor of the cave.

<So far I'm fine,> she said, but her thought-speech was shaky. <Still . . . breathing . . . with my lungs.>

But at that moment, two slits appeared in her neck.

Gills.

<*Aaaah!*> she cried.

"Cassie, pull out of it!" Jake cried in an urgent whisper.

<No. No. Almost done. Tobias . . .>

<I'm ready,> I said grimly.

She was tiny. Less than thirty centimetres long. All that was left of her human body were two very tiny doll hands. They made little fins.

Cassie flopped wildly. Her mouth gasped silently.

"Go!" Jake said.

I closed careful talons around Cassie's squirming fish body, aimed for the small sliver of sky that I could see through the cave's opening, and flapped my powerful wings.

I burst out of the cave into fresh air.

<Are you OK, Cassie?>

<Fish   mind . . . panicky . . . water.   Water now!>

<Hang in there. You've been through this before. You know how it is when you first go into a morph. You have to get control of the fish's instincts.>

<Water! Water! I can't breathe!>

I was about three metres up, racing for the water's edge. Suddenly, below me, a Hork-Bajir.

He looked up and saw me. A bird with a fish in his talons.

I doubted the Hork-Bajir would realize that red-tails don't catch fish. At least I hoped he wouldn't.

I swooped down over the water. The huge Yeerk ship was just lowering its intake pipes into the water. I dropped behind a stand of trees that hugged the shoreline.

<Get ready!> I warned Cassie. I let her go like one of those old World War Two planes dropping its torpedo.

She hit the water with a small splash.

<Are you all right?>

No answer.

<Cassie! I said, are you all right?>

<Y-y-yeah,> she said at last. <I'm here.>

<Are you dealing with the fish OK?>

Again, no answer. Then, <Whoa. Cool! I'm underwater!>

I relaxed. <Yes, you sure are underwater,> I said with a laugh.

<I was scared,> she admitted. <I . . . I know this sounds crazy. But I just keep seeing myself. Fried. With a wedge of lemon and some tartar sauce.>

Chapter 22

Jake was next. He morphed and I flew him over the heads of two patrolling Park Rangers who did not even seem to notice me.

Then came Marco. When I exited the cave with him I practically ran into a big Hork-Bajir. He didn't take any notice of me, either.

Cassie's plan was working. Even with all the Controllers on maximum alert, it never occurred to them that their enemy might be a bird with a fish in its talons.

Back in the cave, it was just Rachel.

<So far so good,> I said.

"Yeah. I guess so."

<Are you nervous?>

128

"I'd have to be crazy not to be nervous. Oh well. Here goes."

She started to morph. I'd seen three others do it now, so it wasn't a surprise to me. But it was still horrifying to watch a friend, someone you cared about, twist and deform and mutate before your eyes.

I don't think any of us will ever get used to morphing. Maybe the Andalites are used to it. I don't know. But I'll bet it creeps them out, too, when they have to change.

I looked away as Rachel began to get strange and hideous.

She was almost completely a fish when it happened.

Crash! Crash! Someone was forcing their way through the bushes at the mouth of the cave.

"Heffrach neeth there." A Hork-Bajir!

"Yes, I see it," a human voice said grumpily. "You know, these human bodies aren't blind. Just because you're in a Hork-Bajir, don't get delusions. Use those blades of yours to hack some of these thorns out of the way."

I heard a sound like fast machetes, slicing away the vines and thorns.

"Better not find anything in here," the human-Controller said. "The Visser will do to you what was done to that poor fool yesterday who let the human escape."

I looked at Rachel. It was too late for her to morph back.

<What's going on?> she asked.

<Yeerks! A human-Controller and a Hork-Bajir-Controller, right outside the cave.>

"Go in fergutth vir puny body. Ha ha."

"This was *your* sector to check. You didn't even notice this cave. Keep getting on my nerves and I'll tell *him*!"

"He gulferch you and eat your lulcath. Ha ha."

Suddenly a human head appeared, followed by shoulders. He was wearing a Park Ranger's outfit.

<We have to make a break for it!> I told Rachel. <Here they come!>

"Yeah, there's a cave in here, all right. There's some kind of a bird — "

I grabbed Rachel, now fully in fish morph. But the human-Controller blocked the narrow entrance.

Well, I thought. It worked with a helicopter . . .

With a rush of wings I flew right at his face.

"What the — " He fell back, beating at the air.

I scraped past him.

The Hork-Bajir slashed at the air with one of his wrist blades. He shaved my tail.

But I was in the air now, and moving faster. Only it was hard with Rachel. The weight of a fish is more than a red-tail can carry easily. And I had already carried three. I was tired.

Fortunately, I was also very scared. Fear can make you strong sometimes.

Ssseeeewww!

A Dracon beam sizzled the air above me!

Unfortunately for the Hork-Bajir who had fired, the Dracon beam did not stop when it buzzed by me. No, the Dracon beam hit the underside of the vast truck ship. A small, neat, round hole appeared in the bottom of the ship. It was too small to amount to anything.

But suddenly the Hork-Bajir lost his interest in me.

"Fool!" the human-Controller cried. "Visser Three will have your head for dinner!"

While they were busy panicking, I dropped Rachel into the water with the others.

<Good work, Tobias,> Jake said. <Be careful up there, my friend.>

<You, too,> I said. <Good luck, you guys.>

I could just barely see them, a small school of fish in the shallows. They swam off and disappeared into deeper water.

As I've told you, there are limits to how far thought-speech can reach. We don't really know what those limits are. But I wanted to stay as close to them as I dared, in case they needed me. Not that there was much that I could do to help someone underwater.

I didn't want to stay right over them. I figured that would look suspicious to anyone on shore. It was hard to figure out what to do. The monstrous bulk of the truck ship was overhead, leaving only a few metres open above the surface of the water.

I decided I had to chance it. I flew under the ship, skimming the dappled water below and practically scraping the metal belly of the ship above me.

It was a very difficult flight. I had to stay almost totally level. I couldn't rise or fall by more than a couple of metres.

<You guys still OK?>

<Tobias? I can't believe you can still thought-speak with that whole ship between us,> Rachel said.

I guess I could have told her the truth. That I was within a few metres of them. But then Jake would have just got all mad and told me not to take stupid risks.

I figured that between the time it had taken through the entire morphing process, and carrying them one at a time to the water, plus now the time spent swimming out to the big intake pipe, Cassie had been in morph for just over half an hour. Jake had ten minutes more, then Marco and Rachel.

<What are you guys doing now?> I asked.

<We're looking at the bottom of this intake pipe. There's tremendous suction,> Rachel reported.

<I'll go first and look around. See what's what,> Jake announced. <Here goes. Whoooaaaaa! Man! Whooooaaa! Yah!>

<Jake! Jake, are you OK?> Cassie cried.

<Oh, yeah! What a rush! They should have a waterslide like that at The Gardens. It's like being sucked up a straw by a giant.>

<Cool,> Rachel said. <I'm next.>

<No, let me look around first,> Jake said. <I seem to be in some kind of big tank. It's not very deep. At least not yet. It's filling up. With these lame fish eyes I can't see beyond the surface of the water very well. But I think up in the ceiling there's an opening. Like a grate or something.>

<Up on the ceiling? How are we going to get up there?> Marco asked.

<Well, I think if they fill this whole tank, we'll be near the top eventually. We should be able to morph to human, let ourselves out, then morph into something more dangerous than our human bodies.>

<Excuse me,> Marco said. <But does anyone else ever stop to realize that some of the things we talk about doing are totally INSANE?>

<What? Turning ourselves into fish, so we can

133

be carried by a hawk and let ourselves be sucked up the pipe of an alien spaceship, so that we can then turn into tigers and gorillas and whatever, and overpower the creepy aliens?> Rachel said. <Is that what you mean by insane?>

<That's it exactly.>

<Yep,> Rachel said. <It is insane.>

<Well, OK,> Marco said. <As long as we all know we're nuts. Let's do it!>

Chapter 23

There was nothing to do but wait. Wait while the water level inside the ship rose and carried my friends towards the top of the chamber. Up to where the grate was.

I could not maintain my level flight beneath the ship any longer. I said good-bye to my friends and zoomed out the far side. The open air was a blessing. I soared high on a nice thermal pattern created by the ship itself. I rose high up and over the top of the ship.

The Park Rangers were all around on the ground. The helicopters and two of the Bug fighters were still parked on the ground in the little clearing. The Blade ship was there, too.

Two other Bug fighters continued zipping around at treetop level.

While I watched, they brought the Hork-Bajir who had carelessly fired off the Dracon beam. They dragged him before Visser Three.

We'd got so we thought of Hork-Bajir as these totally fearless, deadly monsters. But this Hork-Bajir was not looking very brave. He collapsed on the ground before Visser Three. I almost felt sorry for him.

It was one of the terrible things about our battle against the Yeerks. See, our enemy was just the Yeerk slug that lived in the heads of Controllers. That Hork-Bajir may have been made a Controller totally against his will. He had lost his freedom to the Yeerk in his head. Now, he was about to lose his life, for something that he had no real control over.

I couldn't hear what was happening down on the ground. But I could see. My hawk's eyes could see far too well.

I turned away. I won't tell you what was happening to the Hork-Bajir. That memory will be my own private nightmare.

But when next I looked, the Hork-Bajir was gone. And in his place was a sudden rush of other Hork-Bajir and Taxxons and humans, all surrounding Visser Three. The Visser looked angry. He was pointing at the sky.

Within a few seconds, the helicopters were lifting off.

The two Bug fighters powered up and took off.

I had a very bad feeling that I knew what had happened. The doomed Hork-Bajir had told Visser Three about the bird he had fired at. And some other Controller had probably said, "Oh, yeah, I saw a bird acting suspiciously, too." And someone had no doubt said, "Hey, wasn't it a bird that distracted the Hork-Bajir yesterday and let that human get away?"

Visser Three had put two and two together. An animal acting unlike an animal meant just one thing to him: Andalites in a morph.

I guess I should have been flattered that Visser Three believed we Animorphs were true Andalite warriors. But it didn't make any difference whether he thought I was an Andalite or a human. He was sending his creatures into the sky. Looking for a bird that was no bird.

Me.

A Bug fighter skimmed over the trees. Its twin Dracon beams fired again and again in short, sharp spears of burning light.

My heart was in my throat. They were killing every bird they saw!

The hawk! This was her territory.

But then, behind me, a helicopter! *Thwak thwak thwak thwak! Ssshhhheewww!*

A Dracon beam. A near miss. I couldn't get away. Between the Bug fighters and the helicopters, they were too numerous, and too fast.

But there was one place no one was going to risk firing a Dracon beam. Not after what Visser Three had just done to the careless Hork-Bajir.

I let go of the air beneath my wings and dropped. Down, down, down. Towards the vast truck ship, spread below me like a steel meadow.

In an instant they were all on me. But the angles were wrong. I was too close to the ship. They couldn't fire!

I landed on top of the hovering ship. I planted my talons on the hard, cold metal surface. It stretched in every direction around me. The surface curved down and away from me so that I couldn't even see the edges. It was as if I were standing all alone on a metal moon. Over my head hovered helicopters and Bug fighters. I could see human and Hork-Bajir and Taxxon eyes all focused on me.

I knew the look in their eyes. The look of the predator.

And me, their prey.

Chapter 24

It was not looking good for me. If I tried to fly off that ship I would be Draconed ten different ways before I could get away.

It was an eerie scene. I stood on the vast metal plain while over my head they hovered, a swarm of deadly predators.

Then things got worse. A lot worse.

It floated up into my vision like a dark moon — the Blade ship of Visser Three.

It hovered just a hundred metres up. I felt my last reserves of courage beginning to fail.

Tobias, old buddy, I said to myself, *you are not going to get out of this alive.*

But they just all hovered there. Slowly I began

to realize the truth — they didn't know *what* to do about me. They couldn't shoot me without hitting the ship.

<Andalite!>

The voice in my head made me reel. I almost took wing out of sheer fright.

He had never spoken directly to me before. It was a voice of such absolute power. Such utter confidence. The mere silent sound of it in your head makes you want to obey. Makes you quiver and fear. It is the voice of dread. The voice of destruction.

<Andalite. Fool. Do you think I don't know what you are? A true bird would fly away.>

Say nothing! I ordered myself. Nothing! If I tried to reply, he might know me for a human. I would not tell him that. I would not give him *anything.*

I closed my mind. But I could not shut out that dark voice.

<Give yourself up, Andalite. I will give you a quick and painless death. As soon as you tell me where the others are.>

I had seen what Visser Three did to the Hork-Bajir who displeased him. The memory was fresh in my mind.

<Have it your way, Andalite. I am patient. I can wait here for as long as it takes. And then you will die. Maybe quickly by Dracon beam. Or,

140

perhaps, if we can snare you, more slowly here in my Blade ship. Much more slowly.>

Just then, I heard another voice in my head. A very different voice. It was faint. As if it were far away.

<Tobias? Tobias, can you hear me?>

Rachel!

<Yes, I can hear you!>

<Tobias! We're trapped! The tank is full, but the grate won't open. Cassie and Jake have already morphed back to human, but they can't get it open. We're trapped in here!>

<Rachel! I . . . What can I do?>

<We can't get out,> Rachel cried. <Listen to me, Tobias. We're trapped. There is no way out. This ship will take off soon. They'll find us when they get to the mother ship and unload the water. Tobias? We . . . we don't want to be taken alive.>

My blood ran cold. My head was whirling. <What are you talking about?>

<Listen, Tobias, we can't be taken alive! Do you understand? If there's anything you can do . . . anything!>

<Rachel! What can I do? I can't get you out of there!>

<I know,> Rachel said. <We *all* know. But if there's some way to . . . if the ship could be destroyed. We know it's probably not possible. I . . . just if there was some way — >

141

<No! No!>

<I have to morph to human. We'll tread water here. We have to be ready for when we get to the mother ship. Then we'll morph into other animals and go down fighting.>

<This can't be happening,> I cried. <This can't be happening!>

<I guess Marco was right all along,> Rachel said sadly. <I guess it always was insane to think we could fight the Yeerks.>

<Rachel . . . I never told you . . .>

<You didn't have to, Tobias,> she said. <I knew. Good-bye.>

She fell silent. In my mind I could picture her regaining her human shape. Treading water with the others, unable to escape. Expecting only the worst. Praying that I might find a way to make their end swift. As Visser Three had offered to make mine.

We had lost. The Yeerks had won, finally. And when we were gone, the last hope of the human race would die.

Above me the Blade ship waited like . . . like a hawk watching a rabbit. Ready to swoop down and finish me.

Only I wasn't a rabbit.

Visser Three was a predator? Well, so was I.

And I no longer had anything to be afraid of. If my friends were to die in the mother ship, I would be lost and alone in a world where I belonged nowhere.

I had nothing more to lose.

Just then I saw something that should have terrified me. Across the metal plain of the ship they crawled and slithered towards me. All around me. A dozen of them. Giant worms. Ugly Centipedes with a hunger for living flesh.

Taxxons.

They had come from the inside of the ship on Visser Three's orders.

If I stayed put, they would catch me. If I flew, the hovering Yeerk ships would fry me.

The Taxxons closed the circle around me.

<It looks as if you have run out of time,> Visser Three said in my head. He laughed. It was not a nice laugh.

Ah, Visser Three, you ruthless predator, I thought. *Very clever. You have me trapped. Trapped like a rabbit.*

But a trapped rabbit is one thing. And a trapped hawk, a hawk with the mind of a human being, is a whole different matter.

The nearest Taxxon levelled a hand-held Dracon beam at me. He watched me with two of the circle of red globs they have for eyes.

I pushed off with my feet. I beat the air with my wings.

I flew straight for those red jelly eyes.

143

He raised one of his feeble forearms to shield his eyes. The wrong move! I trimmed a shade right, raked my talons forward and struck like I was hitting a mouse in a field.

My talons closed around the Dracon beam. The Taxxon's weak grip was no match for my speed. The Dracon beam tore loose from his grip.

<Get him!> Visser Three cried. I could practically see the Blade ship rock from the force of his rage.

But I did not take to the air. I flew fast but hugged the surface of the ship's metal curve. They could not hit me without hitting their precious ship.

I knew just where I wanted to go. Wingtips actually hitting the ship on each downstroke, I raced towards the ship's bridge. Towards the tiny windows where I had seen the Taxxon crew.

I could not save my friends, perhaps. But I could try to grant Rachel's last wish. I could try to bring this ship down.

Even if it meant the end of my friends.

Chapter 25

<|Take off! Move!> Visser Three commanded the crew of the truck ship.

Almost immediately, the huge thing began to move forward. Very slowly at first. But as it moved, it created a headwind. The bridge was moving away from me. The ship was rising as it went. Thirty metres up now. Sixty!

<Ha! Not so easy, Andalite!>

Right then I had a powerful urge to shock the evil monster and say, <Guess what, creep? Not an Andalite at all. The name is Tobias!>

But I wasn't ready to start bragging. The truth was, it was looking bad. The ship was slowly picking up speed.

I flapped harder, harder. I gained again. But it

145

was painfully slow. I was wearing out. The Dracon beam weighed me down. The headwind was building.

Ahead of me, just a few metres away, I saw the bulge of the bridge.

I gained a metre. Another. Another.

I landed and folded my wings. I couldn't fly any more. But I could still pull myself along with my talons, gripping the small edges and ridges that ran along the top of the ship's bridge.

I was there! Below me, transparent plastic. I could see the crew on the bridge. Taxxons stared wildly up at me.

With one desperate lunge I propelled myself into the air. I had to fly full force to stay ahead of the onrushing windows of the bridge.

Then, with one sharp talon, I pulled the trigger on the Dracon beam.

<Fry, you worms!>

There was no recoil. Not like a regular gun at all.

But a beam of intense red light lanced from me to the bridge. It burned a hole through the window, sliced through a fat Taxxon, and began slicing up control panels and instruments like a hot knife going through butter. I squeezed that trigger for as long as I could.

At last, exhausted, I could do no more.

The Dracon beam slipped from my talon and

plunged towards the earth below.

But I had done it.

It was an incredible and terrible thing to see. The ship, big as a skyscraper, vast beyond belief, shuddered as though it had hit a speed bump.

Still it rose, sharply upward into the sky, as if it were a whale breaching. It aimed for space, its natural home. But it was clear that it was no longer under control. It rolled suddenly on to its side.

BOOM! A ball of orange flame!

The out-of-control ship had smashed recklessly into one of the helicopters. The chopper fell in ruins.

The Bug fighters and the Blade ship scurried quickly out of the way. But too late.

KA-RUNCH! BA-BOOM!

One of the Bug fighters had slammed into the side of the ship. The Bug fighter was finished. The Blade ship and the remaining Bug fighter withdrew quickly.

And then I saw the hole.

A tear thirty metres long had been opened in the side of the truck ship. From the hole, the water of the lake gushed. It was a waterfall from the sky. Millions of litres haemorrhaging out.

<Oh, boy,> I whispered.

We were maybe three hundred metres up over the forest now, when I saw them.

Cassie first. Then Rachel and Marco together. And Jake. They fell, fully human, from the torn side of the ship.

They plummeted, helpless, doomed, to the uprushing ground!

<Noooo!>

I knew there was nothing I could do. I *knew* it. But still I hurtled after them. Hurtled with all my speed to them as they fell, arms flailing, mouths open in screams of terror.

Chapter 26

They fell.

But as they fell, they began to change.

Cassie was the first. Feathers sprouted from her skin. One of her morphs was an osprey. A distant cousin of the red-tails.

She fell, and as she fell, she became less and less of a human.

Marco and Rachel had both previously morphed bald eagles. Bald eagles are huge birds, much bigger than red-tailed hawks.

As I watched, long wings replaced their flailing arms.

Jake had morphed a peregrine falcon. Peregrines are so fast they make red-tails look like they are standing still.

As I watched, a peregrine's beak grew from Jake's mouth.

Not enough time. Not enough time! They would hit the ground before —

Shwoooop!

Cassie opened her wings and skimmed above the treetops. Marco barely made it. He fell down into the forest, out of sight. I was sure he had been too late.

But then, up from the trees floated a bird with a two-metre wingspread and a proud white head.

<YES!> I cried.

In the sky overhead, the huge truck ship stopped climbing. It rolled again, on to its back this time, and plunged back to Earth.

<Man, that was WAY too close!> I heard Marco yell. <That does it. I have had it with this Animorphs stuff!>

<You're not safe yet!> I told him. <Look!>

With the truck ship out of the way and falling to Earth, the Blade ship and the Bug fighters came after us.

<Quick! Into the trees! Out of sight!> I yelled.

Like a well-trained fighter squadron, we swooped down into the forest. Down below the tops of the trees, where the Yeerks could no longer see us.

BOOOOOM!

An explosion like a bomb going off. The truck

ship had hit the ground.

The concussion rolled us over like a tidal wave of air.

I rocketed into a tree, but was able to avoid being hurt. <Everyone OK?> I yelled.

One by one they said yes.

But the explosion had disturbed every animal in the forest. The birds had all either hidden or flown away during the earlier fighting. Those few birds still left now took wing, startled.

I saw her take off. The hawk. She was scared and wanted to run to the sky.

But the sky was not a sanctuary for her.

I don't know which ship fired the Dracon beam. Whether it was one of the Bug fighters, or the Blade ship.

You see, they'd had a good long look at me. And she looked just like me.

The Dracon beam sizzled. It burned off a wing.

And she fell to Earth, never to fly again.

Chapter 27

The Yeerk truck ship burned. What was left was eliminated by the Yeerks. No evidence was left behind. No proof that we could show to the world.

But we had destroyed it. And a Bug fighter as well. And we had got out alive.

Most of us.

It was a day later when I went to see Rachel again. It was like she was expecting me.

"Hi, Tobias," she said. "Come in. It's safe."

I hopped through the window and fluttered over to the dresser.

"How are you doing?" she asked.

<I'm OK,> I said.

She looked unsure of what to say next. "Look,

um, Tobias . . . maybe this seems crazy. But Cassie and I were thinking, you know, that maybe we'd go back up to the lake. Try and find . . . her body. The hawk. You know, and at least bury her."

<No, that doesn't sound crazy, Rachel,> I said softly. <Not crazy at all. Just human.>

She looked keenly at me. "Well, we are human. *All* of us."

<Yes. I knew I was human when I realized how . . . how sad I was that she was killed. See, a hawk wouldn't care. If she had been my mate, I would have missed her, been disturbed. But sadness? That's a human emotion. I know it seems strange, but I guess only a human would really care that a bird had died.>

"If you helped us look, maybe we could still find her body."

<No. Her body will be eaten. By a raccoon, or a wolf, or another bird. Maybe even another hawk. That's the way it is.>

"That's the way it is for wild animals, Tobias. Not humans."

<Yeah. I know. That's how I know that you are wrong, Rachel, at least partly. I *am* a human, yes. But I am also a hawk. I'm a predator who kills for food. And I'm also a human being who . . . who grieves, over death.>

She looked terribly sad. She's very human, my friend Rachel.

I went to the window. It was a beautiful day outside. The sun was bright. The cumulus clouds advertised the thermals that would carry me effortlessly to the sky.

I flew.

I am Tobias. A boy. A hawk. Some strange mix of the two.

You know now why I can't tell you my last name. Or where I live. But someday you may look up in the sky and see the silhouette of a large bird of prey. Some large bird with a rending beak and sharp, tearing talons. Some bird with vast wings outstretched to ride the thermals.

Be happy for me, and for all who fly free.

Don't miss . . .

ANIMORPHS

ANIMORPHS 4:

The Message

by K.A. Applegate

<You know, I hate to sound like the only sensible person — so to speak — > Tobias said, <but you aren't here to fight sharks!>

<He's right,> I agreed. <Dolphins don't attack sharks unless the sharks attack first.>

<Wait . . . I'm getting more echoes,> Rachel interrupted. <There's more than one shark. And there's something bigger, too.>

I reached out with my echo-location sense and "felt" the sea ahead of me. <You're right,> I said. <Several sharks. And a *great one*.>

<A what?> Tobias asked.

I was confused. What *did* I mean? The words *great one* had just popped into my mind. <I mean there's a *whale*. A whale. Being attacked by sharks.>

<A great one being attacked?> Marco asked. He sounded upset. It was strange, because we were all upset. More than we should have been.

<You guys do what you want,> Rachel said. <I'm going in.>

We were steaming through the water when I caught sight of my first shark. He was bigger than me, maybe four metres long, with faint vertical stripes.

He was too excited by the hunt to notice me. Until it was too late. With every bit of speed and power I could get from my tail, I rammed the tiger shark in his gill slits.

WHOOOOMP!

It was like hitting a brick wall. My beak was strong, but the shark was made of steel or something.

I fell back, dazed. But as I tried to collect myself I saw that a trail of blood was billowing from the shark's gills.

Suddenly, from the murky depths, Jake and Rachel zoomed upward, like missiles aimed at the sharks.

WHOOMP! Rachel hit her target.

Jake's shark twisted just in time. Jake

scraped across the shark's sandpaper skin, and before he could get clear, the shark was after him.

<Jake! He's on your tail!>

<I got him!>

<Look out! Coming up on your left, Marco!>

They were as fast as we were, they were as manoeuvrable as we were, and the sharks had one terrifying advantage — they did not know fear.

It suddenly occurred to me that we might lose. We might be killed.

<Marco?>

<I . . . I think I'm hurt,> he said.

I looked for him. He was drifting in the water, almost motionless, twenty metres away. We all swam over, crowding around him.

Then I saw the wound. I think I would have screamed, if I could have. His tail had almost been bitten off. It was hanging by a few jagged threads. It was useless.

We were way out in the ocean. And Marco could not hope to swim back. . .

And coming soon . . .

ANIMORPHS

ANIMORPHS 5:

The Predator

by K.A. Applegate

The first thing that happened was the fur. It sprouted quickly from my arms and legs and all down my body. Thick, rough, ragged, black fur. It grew long on my arms and back and head. It was shorter everywhere else.

My jaw bulged forward. I could hear the bones in my jaw grind as they stretched and the non-human DNA changed my body.

With this morph I had arms, as usual. Only they were a lot bigger. A *lot* bigger. My legs bent forward. My shoulders grew so massive it was like having a couple of pigs sitting on my back. I also had an enormous round belly and a leathery chest.

My face was a black, bulging, rubbery mask, and my eyes were practically invisible beneath my heavy brow.

I had become a gorilla.

Further down the alley, the thugs had lost patience with the old man.

"Let's just kick his butt," one of the geniuses said.

That's when I decided to say hello. To get their attention, I picked up the dump-bin and threw it against the far wall of the alley.

Yes, a full-sized dump-bin.

CRASH! BOOM!

"What was that?"

"Look! What *is* that thing?"

"Whoa! That's some kind of a . . . of a monkey!"

Monkey! I thought. *Excuse me? Monkey? I'll show you monkey.*

Before they could decide what to do, I charged. Knuckles scraping the dirty ground, small hind legs propelling me forward, I charged. If they thugs had had any sense they would have run.

They didn't

"Get it!" one yelled.

I grabbed him around his arm with a massive

fist. I lifted him straight off the ground and threw him over my shoulder.

"Aaaaaaahhhhh!"

BOOMPH!

He landed on the ground behind me. The other two rushed at me, one on the left, one on the right. I saw a knife glittering. The knife slashed my arm. It almost hurt.

"Hooo hooo hrrrraaaawwwwrr!" I yelled, in pure gorilla.

With my injured arm, I landed a backhand blow to the knife guy's chest. He flew back. I mean, *flew*. He hit the wall and dropped.

I just grabbed the third guy by the shirt collar and threw him into the dump-bin.

"Don't kill meeeee!" he cried as he sailed through the air.

I had no intention of killing anyone. I hoisted the knife guy into the dump-bin with his friend. He wasn't breathing real well, but I figured he'd survive.

Hah, I thought. *Who needs Spiderman, when Marco is on the case?*

While I was telling myself just how cool I was, I heard the sound.

It was a click. Two clicks, actually. The sound of an automatic pistol being cocked . . .

HIPPO GHOST

ᕼIPPO GHOST

Beware! This House is Haunted
Jessica is sure one of her stepbrothers wrote the
note. But soon there are more notes ... strange
midnight laughter ... floating objects... Perhaps
the house really is haunted...
Lance Salway

This House is Haunted Too!
It's starting all over again. First the note, and now
strange things are happening to Jessica's family...
The mischievous ghost is back – and worse than
ever. Will they never be rid of it...?
Lance Salway

The Children Next Door
Laura longs to make friends with the children
next door. When she finally plucks up courage,
she meets Zilla – but she's an only child. So who
are the other children she's seen playing in next
door's garden...?
Jean Ure

Reader beware – you choose the scare!

Give Yourself Goosebumps

A scary new series from R.L. Stine – where you decide what happens!

Choose from over 20 scary endings!